About the Author

Dr. Arthur Fournier is a Professor Emeritus of Family Medicine and Internal Medicine at the University of Miami Miller School of Medicine. His career has been dedicated to caring for the poor, both in South Florida and in Haiti. His charitable work in Haiti began in 1994. Since then, he has made over two hundred trips to Haiti, supervising medical students, establishing a community health program in Haiti's Central Plateau, and a Family Medicine Residency Training Program. He has published two prior works on Haiti – *The Zombie Curse* and *Vodou Saints*. He donates the proceeds of his books to humanitarian work in Haiti.

Hope Makes Us Live! Hope Makes Us Die! *Lespwa Fe Viv! Lespwa Fe Mouwi!* Heroes, Villains, and Desperate Times. Haiti, 2005–2023

Arthur M. Fournier, M.D.

Hope Makes Us Live! Hope Makes Us Die! *Lespwa Fe Viv! Lespwa Fe Mouwi!* Heroes, Villains, and Desperate Times. Haiti, 2005–2023

Olympia Publishers
London

www.olympiapublishers.com
OLYMPIA PAPERBACK EDITION

A CIP catalogue record for this title is available from the British Library.

ISBN: 978-1-80439-482-3

This is a work of creative nonfiction. The events are portrayed to the best of the author's memory. While all the stories in this book are true, some names and identifying details have been changed to protect the privacy of the people involved.

First Published in 2023

Olympia Publishers
Tallis House
2 Tallis Street
London
EC4Y 0AB

Printed in Great Britain

Dedications

This book is dedicated to Marie Chery, our heroine in the Central Plateau; Dr. Andre Vulcain for his tireless efforts to train Haitian doctors in the art of Family Medicine, and Dr. Paul Farmer for his inspirational dedication to Haiti's poor.

Acknowledgements

To my sources, who must remain anonymous.

"Poor Haiti, one thing after another. They are a people who are suffering. Let us pray, pray for Haiti. They are good people, good people, religious people. But they are suffering much."

– Pope Francis, during his General Audience, 15 December 2021

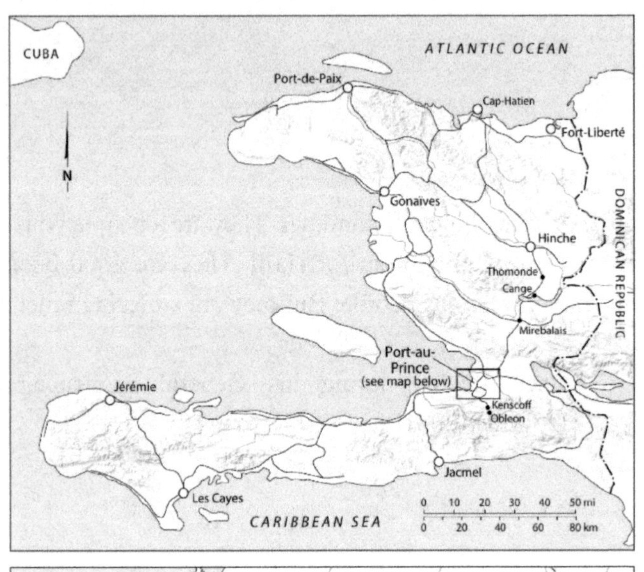
CUBA
ATLANTIC OCEAN
Port-de-Paix
Cap-Hatien
Fort-Liberté
N
Gonaives
Hinche
DOMINICAN REPUBLIC
Thomonde
Cange
Mirebalais
Port-au-Prince
(see map below)
Jérémie
Kenscoff
Obleon
Jacmel
Les Cayes
CARIBBEAN SEA
0 10 20 30 40 50 mi
0 20 40 60 80 km

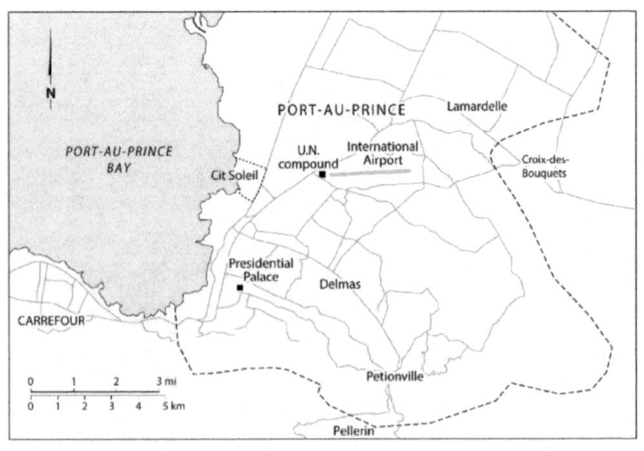
N
PORT-AU-PRINCE
Lamardelle
PORT-AU-PRINCE BAY
U.N. compound
International Airport
Croix-des-Bouquets
Cit Soleil
Presidential Palace
Delmas
CARREFOUR
0 1 2 3 mi
0 1 2 3 4 5 km
Petionville
Pellerin

Preface

Lespwa fe viv! Hope makes us live! Haiti is a land of paradoxes, and the title of this book originates in one of those paradoxes. In a country in which few achieve literacy, wisdom is passed down from generation to generation through an oral tradition of proverbs; *Pawol Granmoun,* Words of the Wise Person. In Kreyol, the word for an old person and a wise person are the same, reflecting the value Haitian culture places on their elders.

For a people whose history is one of enslavement, inequality, and injustice, it is hope that keeps alive their will to survive. The litany of disasters afflicting Haiti has reached extraordinary proportions in recent history. This crescendo of calamities raises the question, "Why do so many bad things happen to the good people of Haiti?" For those who think that all can be explained by random collision of molecules, this becomes a trivial question, with trivial answers, such as "it's just bad luck" or "those people just can't seem to get a break!" These explanations were voiced by friends, colleagues, and the media after the most recent earthquake, the assassination of President Jovenel Moise, and the border crisis that followed.

Another theory, often proposed without evidence, is that the victims themselves are somehow to blame – that it was something they did that caused their fate. For those who look for meaning beyond the trivial, be that supernatural or material, the misfortunes that have afflicted the people of Haiti pose deeper questions: why does evil exist on such a massive scale in places like Haiti and how can we understand and effectively address those evils?

There is certainly truth to the idea that material causes – for example, the extreme poverty, inequality, and corruption that exists in Haiti – provide rational answers to the question of why evil exists to such a large degree there. But is that all there is? Haitians, not the elite of Port-au-Prince, but the Vodouisants living timeless traditional lives in the countryside, and the displaced poor living in squatter settlements on marginal land in the cities – are the Beatitudes personified; humble, peaceful, and perpetually hungering and thirsting for justice. Yet their entire history, from their ancestors uprooting from Africa, their suffering as slaves, and the recent catastrophes of earthquakes, cyclones, cholera, kidnappings, gang violence, and assassination defy any hope for the existence of cosmic justice.

The stories told here surfaced during my work alongside Haitians to improve their health under the auspices of a non-governmental organization I cofounded; Project Medishare in 1994. These stories take place in 2005, a year of anarchy that followed the ousting of President Aristide; 2010, the year of the catastrophic earthquake and cholera epidemic, and 2021, a year which witnessed the assassination of President Moise and its tragic aftermath. These years are key to understanding not only Haiti's descent into a failed state but also the inadequacy of U.S. and international policies and programs to respond to these crises. The year 2005, which showed so much promise as Haiti prepared to celebrate its bicentennial, ended with a surge of kidnappings, drug trafficking, and gang violence.

Those evils have resurfaced again this year, following the assassination of President Moise.

An earthquake devastated Haiti's capital and the regions around it in January 2010, followed ten months later by an outbreak of cholera. International aid poured into Haiti along with the promise of foreign donors that Haiti would be rebuilt. Free primary education was declared for all Haiti's children. However, most of those dollars ended up in the hands of contractors, foreign N.G.O.s and international aid agencies, with little trickling down to the people who needed them.

Tensions mounted in 2020 as plans for a presidential election were disputed. President Moise lacked popular support, but in the absence of a functioning senate, ruled by decree. He appeared ready to rule by decree for at least one more year when he was assassinated in July 2021. The search for his killers, muddled by infighting and political intrigue, has been put on hold as Haiti was struck by another earthquake, destroying tens of thousands of homes on the southern peninsula and claiming untold numbers of lives. At the same time, thousands of Haitian expatriates are pressing for entry into the U.S. along our border with Mexico or buying dangerous journeys in overcrowded sailboats attempting to reach the promised land known as Miami.

There has been a long-held belief by some (originally the French and more recently by the American evangelist, Pat Robertson) that Haiti is cursed because of a Faustian pact the revolting slaves made with the Devil to drive out the French. As we shall see, however, there is no need to invoke Satan as an explanation for Haiti's woes. Often, there are more human devils to blame.

Through all of this, most Haitian people held to their

belief that all this misfortune was God's will and that somehow good would spring from all this evil. It is no coincidence that in Kreyol the same word "*miwak*" (from the French "miracle") means both a disaster and an event of wondrous good fortune.

We all must find our own answers to the question as to why there is evil in the world. However, there are lessons to be learned on this subject from the true-life experiences and moral choices of the heroes and villains of the stories that are captured in this book. The first is a remarkable tale of a kidnapping and rescue in 2005. Next are stories of heroism and triumph over adversity in response to the earthquake and cholera epidemic of 2010. Finally, we will look at the assassination of President Moise, the hidden forces that led to his murder, and the disastrous aftermath of anarchy, violence, and failed policy that followed. As we head towards 2023, the humanitarian crisis in Haiti continues to deteriorate. The Haitian government and international agencies (with few exceptions) have proven impotent to stop it. Yet the Haitian people cling to hope. That hope is slowly dying, however. One can only take so much before *lespwa fe viv!* becomes *lespwa fe mouri!* – hope makes us die!

2005: Goatherd and the Lamb

Introduction

It was a writer's dream come true – a story laden with action and suspense – a drama played out by characters who personified the essence of both good and evil, the central question of Theodicy. When I first met the protagonist of this tale, I thought he was a prisoner – brought to our (the University of Miami Miller School of Medicine's) free clinic in Miami's Little Haiti by three men with the letters "F.B.I." embossed on their t-shirts. It soon became clear, however, that he was not a prisoner but a hero!

He was brought to our clinic along with his wife. They had just arrived from Haiti as participants of the F.B.I.'s Witness Protection Program and she was feeling ill – vomiting that turned out to be pregnancy related! Since neither spoke English, it was the F.B.I. agents who first told me the story – of him, a Haitian goatherd, and a child kidnapped by some of the nastiest villains imaginable. As the story unfolded, I discovered just how this improbable goatherd had earned the admiration of these battle-hardened law-enforcement officers.

The story tested even my credulity – though long ago, in the early days of the AIDS epidemic, I vowed never to doubt a Haitian. I peppered the shy man with questions in Kreyol, almost like a prosecuting attorney, looking for a crack or a flaw in his storyline. Instead, the more he spoke the more astounding the story became. Detail after detail fact-checked with each other and resonated with what I know about Haiti and its people. I interviewed him and the F.B.I. agents for hours after the clinic session ended. Later, to be absolutely sure of the story's veracity, I obtained court records of the official proceedings surrounding the kidnapping. These court records proved invaluable not only in fleshing out the facts of the story but also providing insight into the character and motivation of its heroes and villains.

It was a story that begged to be told not just because of the ordeal the kidnapping victim and her parents endured or the goodness of the goatherd. No, it was a story that asked profound questions about the nature of good and evil and the moral choices we all must make. It was a story set in Haiti – in a unique time and place but with universal lessons for all students of the human condition.

Those who are not familiar with Haiti and its people will find that naïve stereotypes or prejudices about the relationships between race and poverty, work-ethic, intelligence, and moral fiber will be shattered. Those unfamiliar with Haiti might come away from this story with the impression that Haiti is a dangerous, crime-ridden place. Not true, at least in the countryside where most Haitians live. Although desperately poor, Haitians are an intensely spiritual people who, like this simple goatherd, do the right thing because that's how they were raised and that's what's expected of them. The worst name you can call a Haitian in rural Haiti is a *volé* – a thief. In rural Haiti, where police are at best absent and at worst instruments of oppression, it is the universal expectation of moral behavior, not external agency, that maintains social order.

Many in the United States see poverty and crime as inextricably linked. In Haiti, however, poverty per se is not the problem. The real source of the kidnapping problem in Haiti (and indeed most of its social ills) is not poverty but a drastic contrast between the life experience of the rich and poor, particularly in the capital, Port-au-Prince. Poverty for most in Haiti's countryside is what the prize-winning physician Paul Farmer terms "decent poverty" – a subsistence existence that at least allows you to feed your kids, send them to school, and gives hope you might survive to a genteel old age. In the countryside, everyone is poor. Crime is a city phenomenon – fueled by the indecent poverty of squatters living in slums and the exploitation of the poor that comes with inequality, exacerbated by exposure to materialistic non-Haitian values found only in urban environments connected to the outside world, such as Haiti's capital. Even in the capital, kidnappings were a rarity in Haiti until they erupted in the chaos and anarchy around the time of the rebellion against and departure of President Aristide when this story took place. Rooted in this particular place and time gives this story a unique Kreyol feel that also sheds light on the consequences of recent events surrounding the assassination of President Moise.

To understand why this is true, one must know something of Haiti's unique history and people. In reality, there are three distinct Haitis. First, "Ayiti" – rural, peasant, Kreyol-speaking, Vodou-practicing, and culturally West African. Second, "The Republic of Port-au-Prince" – dominated by the elite, where French is spoken alongside Kreyol, and Catholicism is practiced alongside Vodou. The third, "Haiti Abroad" – the Diaspora Haiti, is often forgotten when attempting to understand modern Haiti, but it is at least as important as the other two. All three of these worlds collide in this story.

In the eighteenth century, Haiti was the richest colony in

the new world. Marie Antoinette could not have said "Let them eat cake," were it not for Haitian sugar to bake the cake, Haitian chocolate to frost it, and Haitian coffee to wash it down. Unfortunately, colonial Haiti's wealth depended on slaves. The plantation masters were aristocrats. Only male aristocrats went to Haiti, however. Their wives were reluctant to give up the comforts of the *chateau* and *salon*. So, the masters took female slaves as concubines. The male offspring of these liaisons (or, from the slaves' perspective, rapes) were given an education and a role in overseeing plantation affairs. They had money and could even have slaves of their own, but they were not free. Their sisters' lot in life, depending on the shade of their skin color, ranged from mistress to prostitute to household servant. These *"mulattoes"* united with the slaves in revolt beginning in 1793, and finally succeeded in driving out Napoleon's expeditionary force in 1805. In reality, however, there were two rebellions – the African slaves fighting for their freedom and the *mulattoes* waging an almost Oedipal campaign against their fathers.

The sugar plantations of Haiti were centered around the few flat plains near the coastal cities of Cap Haitian, Port-au-Prince, Les Cayes, Leogane, and Gonaives. After the revolution, the *mulattoes* tried to re-instate the plantation economy, but the former slaves would have none of it. They literally took to the hills ("*Ayiti*" means "land of mountains" in the Arawak Indian tongue), in effect, voting with their feet – a rural subsistence was the price they paid for freedom. The mulattoes then became an unlanded aristocracy, each family competing for dominance in the politics of the capital, and income generated by customs fees and family-managed business, to maintain their wealth and position in society.

These two Haitis co-existed in parallel universes until the twentieth century. The invasion of Haiti by the United States from 1915 to 1934 ended Haiti's historic isolation and ostracism from the Western powers, as President Wilson invoked the Monroe Doctrine to protect "U.S. interests" from nascent but growing German investments there. However, the proudly independent Haitian peasants revolted against the occupation. To quell resistance, Marines built roads and bridges into the countryside, allowing the peasants to bring their produce to the capital and, after the Marines left, allowing the elite to extend their political control to the countryside.

With each passing generation, the subsistence existence of the Haitian peasant became harder and harder – ancestral lands had to be divided into smaller and smaller plots. Soil depleted of nutrients produced fewer crops and marginal land on mountaintops, cleared of trees, quickly eroded. By the second half of the twentieth century, the rural economy was collapsing and millions of peasants abandoned their birthright, hoping to survive in the sprawling slums of the capital.

Meanwhile, the "dog-eat-dog" political battles of the capital culminated with the rise of "Papa Doc" Duvalier, a dictator who craftily exploited U.S. fears that Haiti would "go Communist" to extract millions in foreign aid while pitting one element of Haitian society against another. His enemies, mostly from the elite and professional classes, fled whenever possible to émigré enclaves in Paris, Montreal, New York, and Boston. This first generation of diaspora were very different from the "boat people" who fled to South Florida in the '70s and '80s. They took to the sea for survival not politics. Both the first and second wave of Haitian expatriates faced cultures very different from their own – the usual difficulties with assimilation that all immigrants face compounded by the fact that they were Black and Haitian.

If these social dynamics between rich, poor, and the diaspora had been evolving for more than a century, why the rash of kidnappings in 2005? It was a perfect storm for kidnappings that year. As a prime example of the law of unintended consequences, U.S. policies regarding drugs, deportation, and the Aristide government set the stage for the tempest. Drug use has never been a feature of Haitian culture. The relative anarchy of the Aristide years, however, made Haiti a convenient stopover and staging area for drug traffic between Latin America and the United States. Acceptance by the Haitian government of Haitian Americans deported after conviction of minor offenses was a condition of receiving U.S. foreign aid. Many of these deportees had convictions no worse than traffic violations, but they all had been exposed to the mass-media culture of the U.S. Few of them had any knowledge of Kreyol or Haitian culture and some had already been caught up in the drug wars that scourged American cities at that time.

It is well beyond the scope of this story to weigh in on the role that the U.S. played in the forced departure of President Aristide in 2004. However, his departure further polarized the existing tensions between rich and poor and created a chaotic, dysfunctional political climate. In this setting, opportunists found that they could settle old scores. Kidnapping could not only side-track one's political enemies, but also raise cash for patronage, influence, and political campaigns.

The story is, in essence, true; although, I confess to a touch of poetic license for dramatic effect in the action sequences. Names, locations, and some details have been modified and the storyline slightly compressed and altered to protect the privacy of the victim and the security of the goatherd and his family. The thoughts of the protagonist are as he recounted them to me during our interviews. The thoughts of the villains are admittedly more speculative but often supported or suggested by their actual statements in court.

A Few Words About Haitian Names

The names used in this story are obviously contrived. They are, however, consistent with Haitian cultural practices concerning choice of names. The study of Haitian names, like so many aspects of Haitian culture, is a fascinating one. Children are frequently named after saints in the hope of earning that saint's protection. They are also frequently named after biblical, historical, literary, and mythical figures – the recently assassinated president's last name, Moise, is French for Moses. A surprising number of Haitians are named after philosophers – Voltaire, Rousseau, and Augustin are common as both first and last names. The president exiled in 2005's name is French and Kreyol for Aristotle! Perhaps this custom reflects Haitian reverence for wisdom, or perhaps it started with their colonial masters mocking their enslaved ancestors by choosing such fanciful names. The truth most likely stems from both. Finally, there's the issue of first/last name reversal. Many names are first recorded on a baptismal certificate in French by the village priest. The format is last name, first name (*nom / prenom*). However, to parents who don't speak or write French, this becomes the official name – Etienne Joseph becomes Joseph Etienne!

Chapter 1
The Extraction

September 2005
Agnes felt it first before she heard anything. The long flat of the blade pressed cold and hard against her neck, the edge barely teasing lightly just under her chin as she woke, startled from a profound sleep. Nine years old, her day had started in Brooklyn, rising before five a.m. with her parents so as not to miss their flight from Kennedy International Airport to Port-au-Prince. She had fallen asleep an hour before, exhausted from her day's travel, but thrilled to be back in Petionville, reunited with her extended family.

Petionville had changed since her last visit, Agnes thought, as the family's SUV ascended Rue Tabarre from the airport toward the family compound. There were more people in the streets and more car wrecks by the side of the road, not to mention the UN Humvees patrolling the perimeter of *"Ti-Falluja"* – Petionville's open-air market, swollen with market women escaping the chaos and violence of the capital below them. Agnes had heard about *"Ti Falluja"* on the Kreyol radio station back in Brooklyn. Now she saw it with her own eyes.

Petionville, sitting on a broad knoll halfway up the mountain behind Port-au-Prince, used to be considered the home of many of Haiti's elite families. Of course, in addition to their elegant homes, there were shops and markets, so even in the best of times, Petionville streets were frequently clogged with street vendors, pedestrian, and vehicular traffic. But in the spring of 2005, as a rebel army intent on overthrowing President Aristide descended on the capital, its slums erupted in violence.

Haitians' opinions of President Aristide varied wildly, often with the political persuasions and social class of the person holding the opinion. Was he the former slum priest, now champion of the poor, or just another demagogue dispensing power and patronage to uneducated cronies? In 1994, after he returned to his presidency from exile, he abolished the army that sent him into exile after a coup. It seemed sensible to many outside observers at the time – why would a tiny nation like Haiti need an army twenty thousand soldiers strong? Yet the army, along with Catholic Church, were foundations of society in the capital. Lacking an army, Aristide armed and paid gangs in the slums called *"chimeres"* after the mythical multi-headed monster. His opposition did the same. Caught in the crossfire were the thousands of women who sold their wares on Boulevard Harry Truman, just outside Cité Soleil, the capital's largest slum. Fearing for their lives, the market women abandoned their stalls and in many cases their homes, fleeing to the streets of what they assumed was the safest place possible – Petionville.

The throngs in *Ti Falluja* forced the chauffer to detour down Rue Pan-American, then ascend again to Rue Rigaud. Even their own relatively quiet street seemed to have more pedestrian traffic than before. Their truck pulled alongside a pink concrete wall with broken glass encrusted on the top. Since her last visit, a year before, the wall had been spray-painted with graffiti, equally representing the political spectrum – *"TiTid toujou, au bas LaTortue!* (Aristide forever! Down with Torture!) superimposed on *"chimeres tue-nou!* (The chimeres are killing us!)." Pierre, the family chauffer, got out, looked in both directions, and pushed open the large green iron gate.

Once inside the family compound, however, when the gate closed, their home seemed like it had always been – a quiet respite and safe haven from the cacophony that surrounded it – so different from Brooklyn in so many ways. They were greeted by Josette, the family cook, who had a feast waiting for them; rice and beans, plantains, *legume* (vegetables), and *kabrit.* This last item was a delicacy reserved only for special occasions – fried goat – "Purchased in the market and freshly slaughtered this morning!" Josette boasted. After dinner, exhausted, Agnes went directly to bed. She fell asleep to the sound of songbirds singing outside her open unscreened window.

"Not a sound. A peep and we'll kill everyone here," hissed an oddly familiar voice barely above a whisper from behind a mask. As he said this, he cut a piece of duct tape with the blade of his machete and stretched it over Agnes' mouth.

Don't put that tape over my mouth, Agnes thought in a panic, *I have asthma and I'll die!* But it was too late; her mouth was sealed. Her kidnappers wanted to be sure she did not wake her two younger brothers with whom she shared her room.

In the middle of the night-shadows, she made out two others, taller, on either side of the bed, each holding what appeared to be a gun. All three had their faces covered, incongruously by ski-masks. In seconds, they pulled the duct tape off her mouth, yanked her yellow cotton nightshirt over her head, and stuffed its hemmed end into her mouth. Her hands and feet were quickly bound by duct tape and a sheet pulled from her bed to hold her body like an arm in a sling. She wanted to scream, and the cloth in her mouth would not have prevented it, but she stifled the impulse, fearing her brothers might be killed, as the hauntingly familiar voice had threatened. The light sting of the sedative needle in her shoulder lasted just a few seconds. As quickly as she was awakened, against her will, she was asleep again.

Wilson, the knife wielder, led the bundled girl and Auguste softly down the darkened stairs and out the kitchen door. He stopped to scoop two of the three cell phones from their charging cradles on the kitchen counter and placed them into the pocket of his hooded sweatshirt, not bothering to re-lock the double-locked door or re-set the alarm he had disabled a few minutes earlier. He also lifted the keys to the family car. Clearly, Wilson had been here before – the swiftness of the whole raid depended on his familiarity with the house and its security. Next, he led Ogou to Agnes' parents' bedroom. They burst through the door, leaned on the backs of the sleeping couple, Jacques and Rose, and prepared to bind their hands and feet. "We're taking your daughter," Ogou whispered. "If you say anything or call the police, we'll kill her. We'll call you tomorrow. If you want her to live, you'll need to give us $200,000."

"What makes you think I can get that kind of money?" answered Jacques in a muffled voice, steeped with fear and anger. He was a slight man in his early forties. He struggled futilely to throw Ogou off him, but Ogou was large, muscular, and strong. He placed his hand on the back of Jacques' neck and pushed his head into the pillow. With his other hand, he pressed the barrel of his gun into Jacques' ear.

"This does it!" Ogou growled. "If you tell me you can't get the money, I'll just kill you all now!"

Rose started sobbing.

"You better control yourself, lady," whispered Wilson. "This guy is serious. We're professionals! If your boys wake up, we'll have to kill them!"

Ogou had prepared some double nooses which he slipped over Jacques' crossed hands and feet. He yanked the line tight and tied the tail end of the hand-noose around the foot-noose, flexing Jacques' knees and making it impossible for him to move. He then did the same to Rose.

"Remember, not a sound!" he reminded them. Wilson darted to the door – he couldn't leave fast enough, although he did snatch Jacques' wallet off his dresser and a pair of sneakers on the way out! Ogou, on the other hand, strode arrogantly around the bed so that Jacques and Rose could see his physique and know he was serious.

Outside, Auguste, struggling with the dead weight in the sheet, nearly stumbled over one of the poisoned protection dogs in the walled garden as he ran toward the family Trailblazer. He piled in the back with Agnes. Shortly thereafter, Wilson and Ogou (named for a Vodou warrior) arrived – Wilson drove the trailblazer out the gate. Ogou set off on foot into the darkness. In less than five minutes, Agnes was gone.

Chapter 2
Route 102 to Obeon

At the second corner, Wilson pulled off his mask, switched on the headlights, and turned left on Rue Metellus, which led out of Petionville and up the road towards Kenskoff, ten miles to the east.

"Is she sleeping?" he asked Auguste. "I can't drive with this mask, but if she wakes up, you'll have to hold her down so that she can't see me," Wilson said.

"That shot will keep her out for at least two hours. That should give us plenty of time to dump her and let you get away unseen. That's the advantage of having a professional. He knows these things. He thinks of everything. Did you see how quickly he tied up her parents?" Auguste responded with a loud voice, so that he could be heard over the engine noise.

Wilson glanced at the dashboard clock. Two a.m. He was sweating as profusely as a person with malaria. Small and wiry, he was nervous even under normal circumstances. His skin was slightly lighter than pure black, and he had a curious round bald spot on the back of his head, almost like a monk's tonsure – the result of a fungal infection he suffered as a child. In the weeks leading up to the extraction, he had vacillated continuously as to whether to go through with the plan or just run away. Yes, Ogou was a professional, all right, and he had extracted a devil's retainer for his services. He did have to give the devil his due, however. The raid had gone flawlessly and in a matter of days, he would be a wealthy man.

It took about an hour and half to get to Obleon, on the other side of mile-high Morne Kenskoff, the massive mountain behind Port-au-Prince, where they planned to keep Agnes until the ransom was paid. Hiding Agnes in Granthier was Wilson's idea. Ogou had said they would need to hide her in some isolated place, with few people, where no one, family or police, would think to look for her. Obleon fit the bill. It was the village that he and Auguste had grown up in – a small hamlet on the far side of the mountain. The population there was rapidly shrinking. It was never easy to farm there, a mile up on a mountainside, but through the years, since his childhood, it became nearly impossible. Where once there was a modicum of trees and some wells for water, the land now resembled a desert – a place fit only for goats. Even the goats were now struggling. Many of the former inhabitants abandoned their goat pens when they deserted the village, hoping to find work in Port-au-Prince. One of those pens would be a perfect hide-away, Wilson reasoned.

The road up Morne Kenskoff ascended quickly, past the neighborhoods of LaBoule and Thomasville, where the wealthy Haitian families lived, past the villas of the Israeli ambassador and the Papal Nuncio. After the Haiti Baptist Mission, the landscape transformed drastically – no longer urban or suburban, the road snaked and traversed through timeless, rural Haiti, with terraced slopes and small villages linked by intertwining foot paths. Even though it was three in the morning, these foot paths were already filled with market women and their burros laden with produce, trudging their way down to the markets in Petionville and Port-au-Prince.

Music blared out of the Hotel Florvil – a small hotel and restaurant incongruously plopped down into the village of Kenskoff at the summit of the mountain. It was a popular destination for the young elite – a good place to escape the heat of the city.

"Sweet Mickey must be playing," Auguste volunteered. "He doesn't quit playing until dawn's first light."

The pavement ended shortly thereafter. At Fuercy, they turned onto Route 102 and began their descent to Obleon. The car lurched and swayed in the ruts and slammed over rocks. Fearing the jostling would wake Agnes, Wilson put his ski mask back on. When the village came into view, he shut off the engine and the headlights and rolled to a spot where a footpath crossed the road. Silently, he and Auguste unloaded Agnes, the tin pot of food they brought for her, along with a note Ogou had written. They carried her down the path about four hundred yards to a 10x10-foot goat pen, constructed of hand-hewn slats. Wilson lifted the latch and opened the door. Auguste untied the sheet, lifted Agnes, with her nightgown still wrapped over her head, out of the makeshift sack and placed her on her side in a corner of the pen. He then cut the duct-tape that bound her feet with a jack-knife he kept in his back pocket. After fastening the latch, the two scurried up the trail. Before leaving Obleon, Wilson took the money out of Jacques' wallet, then ran up the hill with the wallet and Jacques' pair of sneakers, his stolen booty, to leave them in a small house nearby.

"She's down there," he whispered to the youth waiting inside. "Make sure nothing happens to her. Here, this wallet and sneakers are for you. You'll get paid some real money in just a few days."

He and Auguste then piled into the car and headed back to Kenskoff. They parked the Trailblazer on a dirt side road just outside the village then descended on foot to Florvil to take in Sweet Mickey's last set. They toasted each other with a celebratory Prestige (Haitian beer), using some of the money taken from Jacques' wallet.

Chapter 3
A Lamb in a Goat Pen

Day One – Post-Kidnapping
The stench of goat urine, pungent as smelling salts, roused Agnes from her drug-induced stupor. In the before-dawn shadows, deepened by the darkness imposed by the nightgown pulled over her head, the sounds of goats braying in the distance and their hooves clacking on the rocks were both frightening and confusing. Where was she? How did she get here? She pulled her nightgown off by grabbing it from the inside, freeing her hands and allowing her eyes to start gathering in the shapes and forms slowly emerging from the darkness. Clearly, she wasn't in Petionville. Because of the altitude, almost a mile high, the air was cold and misty. The rocks she lay on were damp. She untied the knot in her nightgown and put it back on, but it did not help much. She started to shiver, retreating into a corner of the rough-hewn pen, where the first rays of sunlight were starting to penetrate the spaces between the rough-hewn slats that made up the pen, seeking some warmth.

She had a headache, a hangover from the shot of pentobarbital, lingering grogginess, and little memory of what happened the night before – just a vague, haunting recollection of at least one familiar voice, and perhaps a few others she had never heard before. As the evolving dawn brought more light, she peered through the slats of the goat pen. What had felt like mist was actually the moisture of clouds being forced up a rocky, barren, deserted slope. She noticed a tin pot with a lid, sitting on a piece of paper. She lifted the lid and discovered a foul-smelling gruel.

I better not eat that, she thought. *It might make me sick.* Then she squinted at the paper. It was a note, written in English: *"Do not attempt to run away. If you do, we will kill your family."*

"My God, I've been kidnapped," she gasped.

Agnes was slight and thin for her age. Her skin was light enough that her freckles seemed particularly prominent. She had led, until now, a sheltered life. Before she began school, her parents had a nanny who watched over her constantly. Her father insisted she attend a Catholic School in Brooklyn – a Catholic education was the best, he insisted. At his daughter's entry into first grade, he already envisioned her going to Notre Dame or Boston College. Her parents drove her to school each day and on rare days that their schedule did not allow, they sent her via cab.

Agnes had overheard her parents discussing the kidnapping problem in Haiti several times in the weeks leading up to their trip, but never thought the discussion would relate to her. Prior to the ouster of Jean-Bertrand Aristide in 2004, kidnappings – indeed, any kind of violence other than political – was unheard of. The first few kidnappings in 2004 had an almost comical air; indiscreet victims traveling with absurd amounts of cash, or kidnappers starting negotiations in the hundreds of thousands of dollars and settling for hundreds. But, in the chaos that was the interregnum between Aristide and President René Preval, kidnapping soon became a growth industry.

Her parents were divided on the issue. Her father, Jacques, scoffed at the idea of changing their plans. "These are just a bunch of thugs, criminals deported from the US, second-generation punks who don't even speak French or Kreyol," he argued. "They prowl a few bad areas around the airport. If Pierre (their chauffer) is waiting for us with the motor running and takes the safe route up to Petionville, we'll be fine. Those who've been kidnapped have been boisterous fools. If we're discreet, nothing will happen to us."

Rose, Agnes' mother, was more cautious. "It's all over the [Kreyol] radio. Everyone's talking about it, everyone's canceling their plans."

In the end, her father won out – they had been coming to Petionville for years and had never had a problem. They had family there who looked forward to their visits. Kidnapping was a temporary phenomenon that would be dealt with as soon as the interim government cracked down on Aristide's *chimeres*. Besides, they had their medical mission to conduct. Once they got to Petionville, they would be secure.

In fact, in their family, Jacques always had the last word. They were a traditional Haitian family, descended from the Haitian elite. Even though both he and Rose were doctors, in their world, he was still dominant – the one who made all the important decisions.

There is a spectrum of attitude towards the poor among Haiti's elite that ranges from "noblesse oblige" to "let them eat cake." Jacques was of the "noblesse oblige" school. Haiti had been good to them; he lived a life of comfort and privilege there and even received his medical education in Haiti for free. "To those whom much is given, much is asked," was his creed.

That is why each year since he finished his training, he shut down his and Rose's practice in New York for a week to conduct medical missions in Haiti – free "open air" clinics for the poor who farmed the mountaintop land near the villages of Kenskoff and Fuercy. One would think such acts of charity would receive universal praise. Jacques was flummoxed, therefore, when some of the other Petionville families criticized him. "You're enabling the failed Aristide regime," they told him. "Let the poor take care of themselves!"

He took immense pride in being Haitian, descended from slaves who threw off the yoke of France. He wanted his children to know this heritage also. He was always telling Agnes that Alex Haley did not need to go up the Congo to discover his roots. All he needed to do was to come to Haiti. No matter that Agnes had no idea whom or what he was talking about. So, despite criticism from his neighbors, he returned to Haiti each year with his family to conduct their "mission of mercy."

Agnes recollected these discussions as she huddled on the eastern side of the goat pen, still trying to warm herself in the rising sun. *I could easily kick out these slats,* she thought, *and there's no one around...* Then she read the note again. *No. They know where I live, and I have no idea where I am. Best to stay put for now... If only I could reach Papi. He'd know what to do.*

When the sun passed about a quarter of the way through its daily arc, a youth appeared in the distance and slowly descended towards the pen. He was carrying another covered tin along with two plastic packets of water. He unlatched the gate of the pen, opened it, and entered, proffering Agnes the tin and water packets.

"Hi, my name is Plato. What's yours?" he asked in a friendly manner. It would be easier on both of them, he thought, if they could have some semblance of friendship.

"Why should I tell you?" Agnes shot back. "Where am I?"

"I can't tell you that," answered Plato sheepishly. "All I know is I'm supposed to watch you and bring you food and water. You did not eat what they left you last night. Here, you might like this better." With that, he lifted the lid to show her the tin was full of hot porridge. Agnes, however, wanted nothing to do with either Plato or his offering.

After several minutes of uncomfortable silence, he placed the tin and water packets on the ground, exited, and re-latched the gate. "Well, it's here for you when you want it," he mumbled awkwardly.

As he started up the hill, Agnes realized that this youth was, in effect, her jail keeper. She called out to him.

"Can't you let me out for a while? This place is so smelly!"

Plato seriously considered Agnes' request. It was true, the pen really had an offensive smell. He really wanted her to like him. But Ogou had made it clear; if Agnes were to escape, he would be held responsible.

"No, I can't take a chance you'll run away."

"How long do I have to stay here?"

"I don't know. There will be some men coming tomorrow. They'll probably know more…"

Chapter 4
The Demand

Rose started screaming as soon as she heard Josette entering the kitchen. "Josette, come quickly to our bedroom and untie us! *Zenglando* (bandits) came last night! They've taken Agnes!"

Josette instinctively went to Jacques first. After all, he was the one who actually paid her. Jacques lay quietly while Josette untied him, embarrassed that their servant would see him bound like a slave. As soon as he was free, however, he bolted to the children's room, followed shortly by Rose and Josette. It was true; Agnes, his favorite, was missing. His sons, aroused by their mother's screams, sat dumbfounded on their beds as he explained what had happened.

"Get dressed," he barked. "We're sending you home on the next plane. *Memé* will take you to the airport and care for you until we can come home."

Rose was in a trance-like state. She had been in a panic since the kidnappers burst in, while vainly holding out hope that the whole thing was just a bad dream. Agnes' empty bed shattered that hope.

A phone ringtone parodying the Marsellaise brought Rose back from her musings. It was curious, she thought, as she picked up her husband's phone, that her phone, which should have been recharging next to his, was missing. Even more curious, the caller ID identified herself!

"We have your daughter," the voice on her stolen cell phone rasped in Kreyol. "We want $200,000 in four days, or we'll kill her."

"That's impossible!" she cried, while silently mouthing and motioning Josette to get her husband from the bedroom.

"No excuses, no delays, no negotiations!" the caller shouted in an angry voice. "I'll call you in three days and tell you where to leave the money." Then, he hung up.

Rose broke out in a sweat and became nauseated. Her heart was pounding and by the time her husband arrived, she was weeping. She couldn't stop herself from lashing out at him. "I told you we shouldn't have come! It's your fault!" she sobbed.

Jacques sat stone-faced while Rose told him the ransom demands. One would think (and, indeed, the kidnappers assumed) that two practicing cardiologists would have a considerable amount of cash at their disposal – enough to meet the ransom demands of $200,000 quickly. In fact, the family had very little savings; they had only been in practice for seven years – a private practice they had purchased from a retiring doctor with a mortgage. It seemed a good investment at the time but drained their monthly cash flow. In addition, they were paying a mortgage on their condominium and tuition for all three of their children at a parochial school. Jacques firmly believing that a Catholic education, preferably from the Jesuits, far outweighed a public one.

He and Rose went online to their bank. Scraping together every dollar, the best they could mount on their own was $50,000. Jacques could ask his brother, also a physician, for a loan, but he was not likely to have any more cash on hand than

Jacques and Rose did. He could also ask the hospital they worked at for an emergency loan, as well as the bank from whom they took their mortgage, but there were no guarantees that they could patch together $200,000 cash in just four days.

While Jacques worked his calculator and phone, Rose hastily packed her sons' suitcases, loaded them in the car and sent them with the chauffeur over to her mother's house, a few blocks away. She took her older son aside before they departed and thrust a wad of fifty-dollar bills into his pocket. "Here, give this to your grandmother. It's for your travel expenses. For the sake of your sister, you need to be a man now; do exactly what your grandmother tells you, no misbehaving! And don't speak of your sister's kidnapping to anyone! Go quickly now. As soon as Pierre returns, we're going to the police!"

The Petionville Police Station sat across the street from Petionville's main square. On the other side of the square is a flower market, to the left the gingerbread-style Kinam Hotel, and to the right the Eglise St. Pierre. Painted royal blue and white, with small windows and only one door. The police station is an imposing, austere reminder of Duvalierian authority that stood in stark contrast to the tranquility of the park and the faded gentility of the old shops and homes that make up Petionville Center-ville.

During the ten-minute ride from their home to the police station, Jacques and Rose explored every possible way to raise the demanded ransom. They had some savings and some family members they could count on, plus the possibility of a second mortgage, if only the paperwork could be expedited. That would be difficult to do in four days, however, with them both in Haiti. At best, they'd come up short by about a hundred thousand dollars.

"We can give them whatever we raise, and they'll probably accept it," offered Jacques meekly, still stung with the accusation that, ultimately, he was responsible.

Rose, however, would have none of it. Either they'd have to find Agnes in the next four days or pay the full amount. She wasn't taking any chances with her daughter's life.

It was eight forty-five when Pierre, their chauffer, dropped them off. The station didn't open until nine and there was already a long line of supplicants wending from the iron-bar gate that blocked entry to the station, down the stairs, and along the sidewalk towards the Kinam. Jacques took a spot in the line while Rose approached the gate, hoping to plead their way to the front of the line.

Behind the gate, in the open doorway and the vestibule behind it, four policemen milled about. Dressed in starched blue and white uniforms with epaulets on their shoulders and stripes down their pants, they were young, lean, and fit. Two carried very large automatic weapons. They ignored the people in the line, as well as Rose's entreaties until nine, when they carried out a table and chair to just inside the gate. One officer unlocked the gate while another, armed with a stack of blank police reports, took a seat behind the table. The other two officers retreated into the darkness of the vestibule.

"Please, take me out of turn, *gendarmes*, I beg you!" implored Rose. "Our daughter's been kidnapped!"

"I can't do that," the office responded in French so that the peasants, who made up most of the line of supplicants, would not understand him. "I'd have a small revolution on my hands. All these people have major things to report. What makes you think yours is the most important? We must have order…"

Rose maintained her position at the side of the gate, hoping the intensity of her stare would somehow hasten the process, while Jacques inched slowly forward in the line. Each interview took what seemed to be an eternity; a series of interminable questions followed by a printing of the response on the police report form. Rose noted the unevenness of the officer's printing and his frequent misspellings. Before she knew it, it was eleven and only four people had advanced to file their complaints, each one placed neatly in the out-box.

Rose returned to her husband. "I think we're wasting our time here," she whispered in English.

"I agree," said Jacques, also in English. "We'll be lucky if we get a report filed before closing. And then what will they do with it? I have an idea. Let's go to the embassy. We are U.S. citizens, you know. They may help us there more than these fellows."

Chapter 5
Morning Report

Omart stared off the balcony of the Montana Hotel. The entire city of Port-au-Prince was under his gaze – the cathedral, the presidential palace, the police barracks. Beyond were the slums of Cité Soleil, Village de Dieu, and Bel Aire. The largest identifiable feature, by far, however, was the cemetery – at least several football fields in size and crammed with a hodge-podge of above-ground tombs; some elaborate, some humble.

There is more to the city of the dead than the living here, he mused.

Omart's jaundice toward Haiti's capital came at the end of a month-long stint in Port-au-Prince as Chief of a Special Operations Unit of the Federal Bureau of Investigation. The unit had been deployed to Haiti after the rush of violence that had erupted after the departure of President Aristide. His unit's job was to protect U.S. citizens. Specifically, they were to investigate all homicides, kidnappings, and robberies and assure the embassy that the victims were not U.S. citizens or in any way related to U.S. interests. The first part of his assignment was easy – the victims brought into the morgue each day were identified promptly by their families who wanted to give them a proper burial. They were overwhelmingly poor Haitians, some gang members, but most merely innocent bystanders, caught in the crossfire between rival gangs and/or UN troops. The second part proved more difficult, for headquarters in Washington saw lots of possible threats to US interests in Haiti – a clandestine return of Aristide, a revolt of the poor, a surge of emigration, and increased use of Haiti as a transit point for drug trafficking, to name a few.

His colleagues in Miami had warned him that Haiti would be a hellhole as a result of all the violence in the capital's slums. Certainly, the morgue behind the University Hospital could qualify as an inner circle of Hell, with corpses stacked upon corpses. The slums surrounding the capital weren't much better; frequently, dawn found the streets littered with dead and dying. Strangely, however, something about this country fascinated him.

Omart did not fit the stereotype of a Special Operations F.B.I. agent. He was quiet, thoughtful, soft spoken, and something of an introvert, although he enjoyed talking to the hotel staff. He used these conversations to learn more about the country, particularly its history and politics. He was even learning some Kreyol; at least enough to order food, get his clothes laundered, and find his way around town.

He was muscular, but not excessively so. Premature baldness made him look older than he was; forty rather than his actual age of thirty-three. He entered the F.B.I. right after college – he majored in law enforcement – and in nine short years rose to the rank of Special Operations squad leader.

Omart was a second-generation Caucasian Cuban American. His parents and grandparents had filled his mind as a child with tales of their island paradise, co-opted by the Cuban Revolution. Looking out from the Montana, he had to believe there were many similarities between the two countries. In fact, if the truth be known, the realities of Haiti paled the stories of his grandparents – the mountains here were taller, the people proud but poorer, more open in their practice of Vodou than the Cubans were of Santeria. In the final analysis, however, his fascination with the country – or more exactly its people – came down to the question of justice.

Growing up, the injustice of the Cuban Revolution was all he heard about. It was why he went into law enforcement. He wanted to bring justice to this world, or at least to do his little part to accomplish that. And then he was assigned to Haiti, and the injustice suffered by the people there smacked him in the face. There were masses of people below him now, hungering for justice. Perhaps, he hoped, before he left, he could make a difference.

As the sun rose, Omart could see the hotel staff arranging the breakfast buffet on the poolside patio below him. He was always one of the first guests to descend for breakfast, lured by the aroma of freshly brewed Haitian coffee and the scent of vanilla and cloves wafting from large bowls of *avione* (Haitian oatmeal). He had become addicted to Haitian coffee, so intense was its flavor – possible grounds for charges of treason from his Cuban-American colleagues, who believed their style of coffee is the best in the world. He looked forward every morning to drawing and savoring the first cup from the pot.

At seven thirty a.m. he was joined by Ed, his second-in-command and Father Rob, for a frequent breakfast ritual the trio dubbed "morning report." A Catholic priest of Irish American heritage, Father Rob had been working in Haiti since finishing the seminary. Although he was only in his mid-thirties, he had already achieved an impressive list of accomplishments; first, founding an orphanage on the summit of Kenskoff Mountain, then a children's hospital in Petionville. He was so moved by the plight of so many sick children that he applied for, was accepted into, and had now completed medical school in New York. Since the troubled time that led to President Aristide's removal, he had been visiting Cité Soleil each day at dawn's early light; providing first aid and medical evacuation to the wounded and last rites to the dead and dying.

For the past few months, it was a predictable morning routine; several corpses to be anointed and one or two survivors who managed to cling to life until he could find them. He took no sides in the battles between pro and anti-Aristide gangs, ministering to all. This earned him the respect not only of the warring factions, but also of the love of the citizens of Cité Soleil. He could walk the slum's paths and alleyways with impunity. He tended to the living first, applying dressings or tourniquets to their wounds, sometimes loading them into his pick-up, which served as a makeshift ambulance and sometimes, if the distance was short, carrying his patients to the triage area of Ste. Catherine's Hospital in the center of Cité Soleil.

His neutrality and good relations with the various factions in the city's largest and most impoverished slum made him an invaluable source of intelligence for Omart and his squad. Father Rob also benefited from these morning encounters. All factions in Haiti's political scene staked out the Montana Hotel. All had paid informants among the hotel staff. It could only help his mission if various factions knew that he was not only under God's protection, but also under the protection of the Federal Bureau of Investigation.

It had been a particularly tough morning for Father Rob –

the two victims he ministered to were both teenagers; one shot in the chest, the other, execution style, in the back of the head. As he consoled the grieving families, he learned that the chest wound victim was a totally innocent bystander.

"It's enough to make you question God's wisdom," he remarked as he re-lived the scene in his mind. "No mother should outlive her offspring. The sad part is, it didn't used to be this way in Cité Soleil. Sure, it was a filthy slum with more sickness and poverty than some entire countries, but it was peacefully poor; people just trying to survive but respecting their neighbors. It used to feel like the beatitudes themselves were being played out in Cité Soleil – a home for the meek, the humble, and those seeking justice. And the funny thing is, it wasn't even policed! Now, it's a war zone!"

Chapter 6
Scramble

After Father Rob left, Omart, his translator, and his chauffeur headed down Rue Pan American for their daily trip to the morgue. They pushed through the crowd of mourners pressing at the entryway as gently and as respectfully as they could, then asked the morgue attendant if they could see the new "arrivals." Indeed, there had been several corpses brought in from the adjacent hospital as deaths from natural causes. In addition, however, there were two bodies being withheld from release to their families pending investigation by the Haitian National Police.

The morgue was little more than a storage room with shelves stacked high with corpses frozen by rigor mortis in the postures of their terminal agonies. The two bodies in question had not been washed or draped. One had an entry wound over his heart. The whiteness to his palms and nail beds told Omart he had exsanguinated every drop of his blood. Both had a glint of oil on their foreheads in the sign of the cross. Clearly, they were the youths Omart had just heard about from Father Rob.

"Don't worry," the morgue attendant told the translator. "They are not U.S. citizens."

Returning to the hotel, even with two more cups of coffee, Omart became intensely introspective – almost in a trance. The sight of the victims, the graphic nature of their wounds, and the wailing of their families outside the morgue made Father Rob's morning report all too real. Perhaps his quest for justice was "mission impossible," at least in places like Haiti – the illusion of its possibility a cruel hoax perpetrated by a harsh, uncaring God.

Around noon, Omart was roused from his reverie by the chirping of his bureau phone. "Get your crew over to the embassy," barked the voice of the officer of the day on the other end. "There's been another kidnapping. This time it's a U.S. citizen. A nine-year-old girl."

Omart rallied his six-person squad, with the help of his bureau chirper. Within ten minutes, the six-man team had piled into a Humvee and descended Rue Pan-American, across Avenue John Brown to Boulevard Harry Truman and the U.S. Embassy. Although protocol dictated a more formal clearance, Security, familiar with the unit and warned of their arrival, waved them through.

The officer of the day, a Marine, welcomed them and invited them into a briefing room. A light-colored couple were sitting there. "These are the Drs. Voltaire," the officer of the day intoned. "They live in Brooklyn and are U.S. citizens. Their child was kidnapped last night."

"We'll do everything we can to find your child," stated Omart, waiving introductions. "What do we know?"

Rose recounted the events of the morning, including the missing cell phones and the ransom call. "They stole your phone so they couldn't be traced," volunteered Omart. The couple looked at each other in astonishment. "It sounds like they've got someone on the inside," he continued. "Any of your household missing in action?"

Jacques and Rose looked at each other, dumbfounded.

"No," they responded.

After an uncomfortable silence, Omart continued. "Can you raise the ransom?"

"It will be a challenge," Jacques volunteered.

"Well, if history is any guide, they'll negotiate. One of us will need to be with you at all times, in case they call again. How much time do we have?"

Jacques and Rose gazed at each other and then at the Special Operations Unit. "Four days," they said in unison. "You have to help us…"

"Tell me more about your daughter," Omart inquired in a low, respectful voice.

"Well, she's only nine years old," Rose volunteered.

"Here, I've brought you some pictures…"

As Omart studied her features, Rose continued. "She does well in school. She's quite smart, actually, and a good child – very obedient! But we've protected her, perhaps too much! She's very innocent – unaware of the dangers of the world."

"Well, that will most likely change forever," Omart warned. "Let's hope she keeps her wits about her!"

Chapter 7
The Good Goatherd

Day Two
Michel awoke at four thirty, as usual, to the smell of coffee, garlic, and cinnamon. He rolled out of bed, pulled on his shorts, t-shirt, and sandals by candlelight, entering the doorway of his bedroom, then stepped out onto the back porch of his traditional two-room home in the small village of Lemardelle. He smiled, kissed his wife Cheri, and thanked her for preparing such a wonderful breakfast – just what he needed for the trip up the mountain. Cheri had risen an hour before him, nursed their infant son, walked to the well down the street for water, and returned to prepare not only coffee and *akasan* (a porridge made from cornmeal, beans, molasses, and cinnamon) and a generous serving of spaghetti, all over a small charcoal stove set up on the porch.

Michel and Cheri's house was made of wood, painted blue and white, with a door and two shuttered windows in front and a door in the back. The gabled peak of the roof had scalloped woodwork and a tiny spear point seated on the crest. These had been the handiwork of Michel's grandfather, who built the home forty years before. Their property was defined by a cactus hedgerow seventy-five feet square – just large enough for a mango tree in the southeast corner to provide shade and fruit.

Their home was in a cluster of small homes at the end of a long, rutted dirt road about a mile from the base of Kenskoff Mountain. Someone from Michel's family had lived there for as long as anyone could remember. There was a time one could raise goats there easily, allowing them to graze and forage in the common grounds between the houses. Over the past decade, however, the area around Lamardelle had turned into a desert – complete with cacti and thorn acacia trees. Michel was forced to herd his goats up the backside of the mountain, where there were large tracts of abandoned farmlands.

Michel was eighteen and Cheri a year younger. They had known each other since childhood, playing together since infancy and flirting since their early teens. Cheri considered Michel somewhat of a prize compared to the other boys in the neighborhood; not only was he handsome, but he also had a sweet disposition and a natural intelligence, even though he was unschooled. In fact, he was much more serious about succeeding in life than his peers who had the privilege of a formal education. Plus, he loved children. He'd make a good father, she thought, when he proposed marriage a little bit more than a year before. When Michel's grandfather died, he left his home and his business – herding goats – to Michel. It seemed like a natural time to start their own family.

Michel rubbed the head of Jean-Peter, his son, perched on Cheri's left hip. She held him there with one hand while she stirred the *akasan*. "*Salu, gwoneg!*" (Salutations, big guy!) he said to his son with mock seriousness. He took great pride in his son – big for his age and, by the consensus of his extended family, destined for greatness. He had two loving parents and a good start in life, thanks to his father's moderately successful enterprise as a goatherd.

Michel kept about two dozen goats, high up in pens, on the south side of the mountain. Each day, Sundays excepted, he carried a sack of *fatra* (mango peels and seeds, garbage and trash) up the hill to feed his goats, turned them loose to graze, and herded them back into a different pen before returning home. His herd was in a good state of equilibrium – with five months of gestation and three months for a kid to mature, if he limited his sales to one goat per month, the she-goats would produce at least one new kid for every goat he sold, and he could bring home to Cheri a steady income of about $35 per month; not bad in a country where the average annual income is $250 per year. It allowed Cheri to stay home with Jean-Peter rather than returning to her work as a seamstress. They were even putting away a small amount to pay for his schooling, still four years away.

The price Michel had to pay for this enterprise was a three-hour trip up the mountain and a slightly less arduous descent each day. On the other hand, the upper south side of Morne Kenskoff provided more extensive grazing grounds for his goats, although they needed the little supplement he carried to them every day. The land was so barren that they could barely survive by grazing only on the sparse tufts of grass and occasional thistles scattered among the rocks and ruts of the mountainside.

After visiting the latrine and saying good-bye to Cheri and Jean-Peter, Michel slung his *macoute* (sack) half filled with yesterday's mango remains over his shoulder, along with a small lunch bag with *dlo* (water), *pan* (bread) and *mamba* (peanut butter) and bounded off to the trailhead to ascend to his goat pens on Morne Kenskoff.

Naturally conditioned by his daily routine, Michel was

wiry and strong, with a bounce in his step and a broad stride. Although the sun had not yet risen, the streets between his home and the trailhead were already brimming with sidewalk commerce and pedestrian traffic. He saluted each shopkeeper, vendor, artisan, and market woman he passed and they, in turn, returned the honor, as is the Haitian custom. He also scanned the gutters of the streets near his home for more supplemental *fatra* (trash) for his goats – discarded banana peels, chicken bones and the like. He scooped these items into his sack without breaking stride. His initial ascent was a little like a fish swimming upstream, so thick were the descending throngs of women and their burros bringing produce to the markets of Croix-de-Bouquets and La Plaine. He took these impediments to his progress good naturedly, wishing each descending woman a good day and offering them a tip of his straw hat.

The traffic thinned after the Obleon trail branched off and the path steepened. If not for the occasional bunch of grass or cluster of thistles, the terrain resembled a moonscape. Michel would gather those thistles if they weren't too far off the path. Thistles were a special treat for his goats! Michel's breathing became a bit labored, but his pace did not falter. As the sun rose higher in the sky, the colors in the valley below changed from forest green to bright green, while the hues in the mountains changed from gold and burnt sienna to desert yellow. As the clouds changed from rose and violet to silver grey, a spectacular panorama unfolded as he ascended – first *La Plaine* and *Morn Kabrit* in the distance to the north, then when he climbed higher, Port-au-Prince, its bay, and the mountainous spine of Haiti's southern peninsula to the south.

The tin sheet roofs of makeshift homes in Cité Soleil, near the port, reflected a harsh light from the rising sun back into his eyes, making him wince. He had cousins who lived there. They came home on Sunday to visit family and pay their respects to the dead, bringing with them horror stories of the transformation of Cité Soleil from a poor but peaceful slum to an anarchic battle ground dominated by rival gangs fighting for control. Despite the effort he had to expend every day to keep his goat business going, he was content with his life and happy to be on the mountaintop daily, with its vistas and breezes, rather than down in the heat, mud, and now the violence of Cité Soleil.

He enjoyed the solitude of the higher reaches of the mountain. As he climbed, he occupied his mind with a variety of pragmatic tasks as well as more philosophic reflections. Despite his lack of schooling, he knew math well; he learned from his grandfather, who told him he would need to add and subtract to care for his goats and to sell them. That particular day, he was counting the days until his pregnant goats would deliver their kids, and how much he might be able to earn when his last batch of kids matured enough to be brought to market. He could not do these calculations without also remembering not just the math he learned from his grandfather, but also the wisdom – passed on as *parole granmoun* – words of wisdom amplified by parables and stories from the Bible and Haitian history. He revered his grandfather and thought of him daily. Even though he was only eighteen, he was already thinking of his responsibility to pass this wisdom on to his own children, starting with Jean Peter.

His goat pen destination for that day was set in a little depression – a geologic dimple in an otherwise uniform ascent to the summit. Michel had built it there to not only protect his goats from the wind and dust that sometimes blasted up the mountain's face but also to hide them from potential marauders, as it could not be seen from the path. As he approached the rim of this depression, he was startled by the sound of approaching voices. Cautiously, he left the path, moving tangentially and slightly upward to a point perpendicular to the path so he could hear them and not be seen.

An improbable trio of men slowly, cautiously descended the path. One, dressed similarly to Michel in a t-shirt, shorts, and sandals, appeared older than the other two, who sported designer jeans, black silk shirts with gold chains around their necks and earrings! Michel had never seen such finery. Their shiny shoes with hard soles made it even more difficult for them to descend, and they cursed each time they slipped and stumbled. Between these missteps, however, they were boisterous and ebullient.

"How did you ever find this place?" asked the taller of the two bejeweled youths to his rustic companion.

"I grew up here," the older man replied. "I used this trail as a short-cut to Petionville. She (Agnes) didn't see me, did she?"

"No, and besides, she's too terrified to recognize you even if she did. After all, we told her we'd kill her if she tried to escape – not just her, but her parents, too," the youth chuckled.

"You won't really kill her?" asked the older man somewhat sheepishly. "I've known her since she was an infant – she played with my own children."

"You better believe we'll kill her if they don't give the full amount, and you too if you have any second thoughts. You're going to get two million gourdes [about $50,000] for your part in this. Think of that. And we're sending a message to every *bourgeois* in Haiti. We mean business. No negotiations with these bastards. They've got three more days."

Their voices started to trail off, but Michel waited until they descended out of sight before heading over the next ridge, towards the pen.

What a strange group and what strange talk, Michel thought. He'd never heard talk of murder in casual conversation before.

Chapter 8
A Reprieve from the Pen

"You didn't eat your food again…" said Plato, as if he were disappointed that Agnes left the second tin cup of gruel untouched. Didn't she realize that he was thinking of her? Being kind? Wilson, a distant cousin, had recruited him into the kidnapping team a few months before, saying only that there was a child who would need a baby-sitter and that he'd be paid well for looking after her. It was important, however, that she not run away.

Plato lived in a small two-room home just about two hundred meters above the goat pen that imprisoned Agnes. He had watched her from that perch all day before. She was a curiosity to him, with her light skin and wavy brown, but not kinky black hair. He hadn't visited her that evening, rationalizing that there was no need to visit, as she hadn't yet eaten the food or drunk the water he had brought her. In fact, he was actually somewhat intimidated by her, with her assertiveness in refusing his offerings. At the same time, he really wanted her to like him.

He walked down to the pen shortly after dawn, the second morning after the extraction, carrying another tin of porridge and hoping his captive would be more receptive to his overtures. He was somewhat perplexed, therefore, that she wasn't at all happy to see him.

"This will make me sick if I eat it. It all smells so foul. I'd rather starve!" exclaimed Agnes, who had decided that death by starvation was better than death by dysentery. She had spent the past day sitting in whatever shade she could find, trying to stay cool and conserve her strength. At night, she huddled next to the slats in a vain attempt to stay warm. She had never been totally alone before. She had always taken the security of loving parents and an inviolate home for granted. She found the experience of imprisonment somewhat frightening, but mostly it infuriated her. She was in no mood to pretend to be friendly to her captor. Defiantly, she hurled the three tins at the rocks on the far side of the pen. The lids popped off on impact, spilling their contents.

"Well, here's some more water, then." Plato thrust a plastic packet of water through the slats of the goat pen almost apologetically. He loved children in general. It seemed cruel to have left her in the pen overnight. He had been told, however, to take good care of her. If anything bad happened to her, he'd been told he'd pay a price.

Food was one thing relatively easy to refuse. Water was something else. Agnes had had nothing to drink for a day and a half. Her thirst was so severe that she was tempted to snatch the water packet from Plato's hand, tear it open, and gulp it down. She had seen these water packets being sold on the streets before and remembered her mother mentioning casually that she should never drink them, as she was not sure the quality of them could be trusted. Such was the power of her will, however, that she feigned indifference.

"I'm not thirsty now," she said, disingenuously. "But I'll take these (the water packets) and save them for later," vowing in her mind to hold off as long as she could.

The next two hours passed awkwardly, with Plato sitting on his haunches outside the pen, staring at Agnes occasionally while she paced back and forth in the pen. Then a group of three men descended from the east. The sun was at their backs, so she could not see their faces. Two lingered behind while the third approached Plato and the pen. He was large and muscular, with a menacing countenance.

For Ogou, the ringleader, every thought and action were a calculated balancing act, intended on the one hand to make sure their plot succeeded and on the other to make sure he was never caught. That's why he left on foot just after the extraction. If caught, Auguste and Wilson would be blamed.

He was brought to the United States shortly after birth by his parents, who had won an immigration lottery. They nicknamed him "Ogou" after a Vodou warrior, hoping that the *Lwa* would protect him on Brooklyn's mean streets. It didn't work. He was taunted by the American kids in elementary school who made fun of his accent and his way of dress. Haitian parents traditionally send their boys to school with slacks, shoes, a shirt and tie. They would never think of sending a child to school in sneakers and jeans. Bullies pulled on his tie and yanked out his shirt. Fights broke out on the playground. Invariably outnumbered, he sustained several severe beatings. To avoid these beatings, he started skipping school. He came to hate being Haitian.

In middle school, he started hanging out with American kids, pretending to be American, not Haitian. By high school, he was buying and selling cocaine. Back in those days, he was casual, almost careless about his dealings. It cost him; he sold cocaine to an undercover agent, was arrested, and imprisoned. In prison, he decided he'd need to be a bully himself in order to survive. He lifted weights and exercised daily, as if he were in boot camp. He picked fights with weaker inmates, knowing he'd be punished by the authorities, but with the calculated upside that he would be feared by his fellow prisoners. Rape proved an even more effective tool for instilling fear in his fellow inmates. In prison, there seemed to be no downside to rape – the guards looked the other way, considering the victims as only getting what they deserved for the crimes they had committed.

He was incredulous when his public defender told him he would be deported, and shocked when his appeal was denied. In 2004, he was deported directly to a Haitian jail in Port-au-Prince. He shared his cell with thirty other inmates. There were no beds, sinks, showers, or toilets. By then, he had forgotten his Kreyol, so he could not communicate with either cellmates or his guards. To survive in a Haitian prison, one needs family to bring food, water, clothing, and bedding. He had no family in Haiti. Flies and mosquitoes buzzed incessantly. Wracked with fever and dysentery, he probably would have died had not fate intervened.

The morning after Aristide left Haiti, all the prison guards left their posts and the prisoners broke out, most headed to the most anarchic quarter of the city – the slum, Cité Soleil. Lessons on survival learned the hard way, Ogou vowed he would never return to jail again. That vow defined his modus operandi as a criminal in Haiti; stay invisible, hire puppets to do the dirty work, be more well-armed and disciplined than the police who might be searching for you or, for that matter, your henchmen, who could always turn on you.

His first few weeks of freedom in Port-au-Prince were difficult; homeless, sick, without money, and not speaking the language, he survived by stealing food from the market women outside Cité Soleil and sleeping under the eaves of some of the more ornate tombs in the cemetery. His fevers got worse, and he collapsed from weakness. A priest who rounded daily in Cité Soleil found him, anointed him, and took him to the General Hospital.

As he was recovering from his pneumonia, he struck up a conversation with a patient in the adjacent bed – a youth named André recovering from a gunshot wound, who happened to speak English. From his dress-designer jeans, silk shirt, and jewelry, Ogou correctly figured that André might have a source of income that was extra-legal. Indeed, André confided that he had a *patron* – a wealthy man who lived up the mountain, who needed men on occasion who were strong and fearless to do things that needed to be done that ordinary Haitians weren't willing to do. He promised to introduce Ogou to his patron after they were released – if Ogou were willing to return to André a percentage of his earnings.

That was how Ogou got started in the kidnapping business. He never met the patron. Instead, he would receive instructions on his targets delivered by couriers. The choice of victims was curious, he thought, not just wealthy people, but on occasion rising senators and deputies, drug dealers, and even servants of prominent families.

This last group of victims was a unique aspect of the 2004–2005 Haitian kidnapping phenomenon. All prominent Haitian families had a cadre of servants, most of whom worked for that family their entire lives. They were often referred to as "family," and indeed often were family, albeit distant relatives. It was a paradox that in a nation born in revolution against slavery, that servitude played such a prominent role in the social order.

From a kidnapper's perspective, servants were easier marks – less likely to be on guard, less likely to be surrounded by bodyguards, obliged to leave the family compound frequently in the discharge of their duties, and easier to negotiate about. Household masters were seen as having an obligation to their servants, almost as if they were their children, and the ransom could always be dropped to some lesser but mutually agreeable fee.

Ogou used the profits from his first few kidnappings to hire young girls as prostitutes and youths to serve as "mules" for drug trafficking. Soon, with his reputation established, a variety of "clients" were seeking out Ogou's services.

Ogou felt it was important to know exactly where Agnes was hidden. What if Wilson or Auguste got caught, or even worse, betrayed him? He also wanted to terrorize their captive – a job he could not entrust to amateurs. Fear, not this shabby goat pen, was what would keep her in his grasp.

He approached Plato silently and saluted him. They had not met before, but there was no need for introductions. He didn't want Agnes to even know his first name; if he were caught, that might come back to haunt him.

He cracked open the pen's door enough to fit his arm in and beckoned Agnes to come over. She cowered in the farthest corner.

"Come here!" he bellowed. "If I have to enter this stinking pen, I'll break your legs with my bare hands!"

Standing up to Plato was one thing, but resisting this thundering hulk was something altogether different.

With that threat, Agnes felt she had no choice but to obey. Once within arm's reach, Ogou grabbed her nightie in his fist and lurched her towards him, slamming her into the gate and pen. "If you dare escape, I'll kill your entire family. Then I'll come after you. You'll be easy to find in these parts, with your light skin. Then I'll kill you, too – but only after I've had my way with you!"

Plato's eyes widened. Now he understood. He was more than a babysitter – he was an accomplice in a kidnapping! Ogou released his grasp and shut the gate. He returned to the other two men and the three of them started down the mountain. As they left, Ogou took a cellphone out of his pocket and thrust it at Plato.

"Here! Do you know how to use it?" he sneered with contempt. It was important that Plato fear him also. "I've pre-programmed it for you. To call me, all you need to do is push the green button. I want to hear about anything unusual."

Agnes sobbed uncontrollably, for what seemed to Plato to be an eternity. He tried to console her, explaining that this wasn't his idea and that he only thought he was babysitting, all to no avail. Then, Agnes noticed a group of children playing a short distance up the hill.

"Please let me play with those children," she implored Plato. "The stench in here is horrible! You can't keep me in here for days. I promise I won't run away! I just want out of this pen! I heard what that man said. If I run away, those men who brought me here will kill my parents and my brothers. They've got guns! You don't have to worry – I'm not stupid!"

She's got a point, Plato mused. If the truth be known, he was feeling more than a little sorry for her – sorrow mixed with remorse for being so naïve. Besides, keeping her in the pen might draw more attention to her than letting her mingle with other children. What if the goatherd picked today to bring his herd of goats here? Wilson and the others thought the pen was deserted. Plato knew better. Before the kidnapping, he had observed Michel's weekly routine from his porch. He just hadn't thought it important to tell them. The trio was now out of sight. He'd just sit under a distant tree and keep an eye on her.

"Just make sure you're back before the sun goes down or if I call for you," he cautioned as he lifted the latch and opened the gate.

Agnes hugged him, genuinely grateful, and Plato returned her hug with a broad smile.

"I'm not a bad person, see… I just need a little money. So don't spoil it for either of us…"

Agnes sprinted up the hill to join the small group of about ten children, ranging in age from five to twelve. The boys were flying kites made out of plastic bags, twigs, and rags. The ridge that separated them from the pen was perfect for kite flying, with a constant breeze fueled by the trade winds forced up the mountain. The girls were singing, with the older girls teaching the younger ones dance steps. Agnes didn't even need to introduce herself, she just joined in the singing and dancing. Later, fatigued by hours of continuous dancing, the girls sat in a circle on the ground, playing *kay* – a game like marbles, except played with small rocks.

Plato settled under the one solitary tree on the hillside, trying to concentrate on Agnes' movements, looking for any sign of suspicious behavior. As the day heated up, however, Plato started to nod off. He had been up most of the night before, anticipating the arrival of his accomplices. By the time Michel bounded over a slight rise, heading for his goat pen,

Plato was deeply asleep.

After overhearing the strange trio, Michel headed up the mountain about another half-mile to the pen where he had left his goats the night before. His herd bleated and crowded near the pen's gate in anticipation. He spread out the contents of his sack a short distance from the gate. When he opened the gate, the goats rushed past him, fighting over the juiciest mango seeds and largest thistles. After they consumed their treats, Michel allowed them to graze the grass in the vicinity of their pen. Once they had finished, he tapped the hindquarters of his lead goat, Christophe, gently with his staff. Christophe, trained in the weekly routine, jumped, then pranced towards the pen that would be their home for the next two nights. The others followed like ducklings following their mother.

Michel always stopped to talk to those children as he tended his goats. He felt sorry for them – their parents were too poor to send them to school – so he always offered a few words of encouragement or professed to admire the boys' kite-flying skills or the girls' latest dance steps. In fact, he knew them all by name, so the presence of a new child was immediately noticeable – particularly this child, with her light-skin and soiled but elegant nightie.

"Who are you?" Michel inquired in a soft voice.

Startled and not knowing if Michel might be one of her abductors, Agnes pointed to the girl next to her. "I'm her cousin!" Her answer provoked peals of laughter from the other children. Even Michel had to chuckle.

"Sure, and I'm President Aristide!" he joked, then smiled gently.

Something about his voice and smile suggested to Agnes

that this stranger might be trusted. The other children seemed to know him, gathering around him while each one tried to hold a finger of his hands. She glanced furtively towards Plato – sprawled under a tree with his eyes closed and mouth open. This could be her only chance. "OK, I'm not her cousin," she whispered almost coquettishly, as she pushed the other children away. "But it's a secret. Come with me."

Michel motioned to the other children to stay where they were. Agnes took his hand and lead him to a spot about ten meters away, that put the other children and the herd of goats between them and Plato, as a partial shield from his view. "Please sit down, you can't be seen by that man over there! I've been kidnapped and if I run away or talk to anyone, they'll kill my family and they'll kill me! Can you help me? If you can reach my father, he'll know what to do…"

"Where is he?"

"At our home in Petionville – 148 Rue Rigaud…"

"I'm afraid I don't know where that is. I've never been to Petionville," explained Michel. "I live down at the base of the mountain, just outside of Croix des Bouquets. I just came up here to tend to my goats. Why don't you just come with me?" he whispered. "I can get you down off the mountain in two hours or less. You can hide in my home until we figure out what to do."

Agnes was torn – she wanted to flee but was paralyzed by fear of Ogou and his threats. "No, they'll kill us all. It's best I stay here."

"How do I reach your father?"

"Well, you'll have to call him. Here, then," she said, as she picked up a shard of unburnt wood and a piece of charcoal from a fire pit beside them. "That's our number," writing in haste as she spoke. "You better go before my guard wakes up."

Michel started over the ridge with his goats, descending a bit, then re-ascending, motioning for Agnes to return.

"Here, take this *pan* (bread) and *mamba* (Haitian peanut butter). I don't know how long it will be until I can return…"

He then circled around to his goat pen – as much as he wanted to help the girl, he still had to tend his goats. They were his livelihood; not just his, but his family's also.

The goats started braying as Michel approached their new pen, first rebelling against their impending imprisonment then scrambling over each other to devour the spilled gruel and to lick the remaining contents of the two spilled tins. The commotion roused Plato from his slumber. *It's a good thing I let the child out to play,* he mused. *If this goatherd had found her, they'd make me kill him. I'm not sure I could do it, but if I didn't, then they'd kill me and her.*

Chapter 9
Darkness Descends

As Agnes watched Michel disappear over the ridge, her heart was pounding. She had never been in danger before and had never been dependent on the kindness or courage of a stranger. Could she trust him? She had no other hope, really, except perhaps to break through the slats after dark and run, run, run, hoping she could find her way back to her family, and hoping her father would know how to protect them all. No, it was best to stay put. He seemed trustworthy, that goatherd, and he promised he'd help.

Unfortunately, as they hastily patched together their plan, Michel neglected to tell Agnes that neither he nor any of his neighbors had a cell phone or the money to buy a phone card. In her own mind, therefore, her rescue would be in a matter of hours – the amount of time needed for him to descend the mountain and call her father to come and get her.

She passed the first few hours after Michel left, therefore, almost carefree. She played for a few more hours with the other children, then hid his peanut butter sandwich in her armpit under her nightie as she returned. Plato, almost reluctantly, locked her back in to the goat-pen, now occupied by two dozen goats.

"I'm going home now," he said with a tingle of remorse or guilt in his voice. "I'll be back tomorrow, though, and I'll try to bring you back something better to eat."

After a while, boredom set in. As the sun set, Agnes studied the goats, deciding which were males and which were females, giving each a name and letting each one lick a small taste of the gruel left in the tins off her fingers. She finished the *pan* and *mamba* Michel left her. Overwhelming thirst forced her to sip a small amount of water from one of the plastic packets she had taken from Plato. It tasted foul, so she spat it out. The sun was setting slowly, bathing the valley below in hues of gold and rose. She pulled off her nightie and used the remaining water in the packet to wash herself. That made her feel better for a short while, but her thirst soon became all-consuming. As darkness descended, she became more and more anxious. With each passing minute, her anxiety grew, fueled by the absolute darkness and the cacophony of continuously bleating goats, braying mules, crowing roosters, and clucking chickens.

"God will always answer your prayers," the good sister at school had taught her. "You just need to know what to ask for…" Until now, she had gone through the motions of prayer nightly, in school, and during Sunday service. If the truth be known, since her world was perfect, there was nothing actually to pray for. Now, the need for God was painfully apparent – someone to make things right, to see that the good are protected and the evil punished. But how could that be best accomplished, given the horrible predicament she found herself in? She would need to choose her prayer carefully.

She arranged some stones she found on the floor of the pen into a cross and knelt before it. "Dear God," she prayed out loud. "If I must die, so be it. Please protect my brothers, my mother, and my father. Spare them from any harm. And so that your justice and mercy might be served, please guide that goatherd to my father."

She repeated this prayer three times – the good sisters had told her three was a lucky number, the number of the Trinity. Then she redirected her prayer to the Virgin Mary. "Go to the Virgin if you really want results," the nuns told her. "God's too busy keeping the planets turning around the sun to keep track of all that goes on in our lives," they said. "That's why we need saints, to intercede on our behalf. And the Virgin, she's the best. How can God say 'no' to his mother?"

Beneath her cross, she arranged some smaller pebbles in the sequence of a heart-shaped rosary, which she began chanting over and over. It wouldn't hurt that her makeshift cross and heart formed a *vevé*, the symbol of Erzilie, the Vodou protectress of families. It was a secret she learned from Josette in their kitchen, as Josette prepared supper. While preparing meals, Josette shared lots of secrets about all things Haitian – the secrets of pumpkin soup and the ancestors and the sacred place Guinea, where she would go when she died. But the most important of these secrets for her as a girl was *Erzilie,* the Vodou equivalent of the Virgin Mary. If she believed in her, and placed her hopes in her, *Erzilie* would be there when she needed her.

That night, the skies opened with a brief but intense deluge – so intense that rocks began rolling down the denuded hillside, banging off the slats of the pen, setting off another round of bleating from the frightened goats inside. It seemed, at first, that God had answered at least one of her prayers. Agnes assuaged her thirst by opening her mouth into the downpour and capturing rain in her cupped hands. The rain stopped, however, after just a few minutes, as abruptly as it began, leaving her drenched but still thirsty. The storm was followed by a chilling wind. Soon, she was shivering uncontrollably.

After wringing out her nightie and using it to wipe off as much of the water off her skin as she could, she rested her head on a she-goat, using her as a pillow and held two kids in her arms for warmth. She slept fitfully, finding it difficult to get comfortable on the rocks or to be comfortably warm, despite the kids in her arms. Worse, with each passing hour, her despair grew greater. Had she made the wrong decision? She had put her faith in a goatherd! Now she was stuck! Now she could never descend the mountain in the darkness and the mud.

Chapter 10
The Wait

Many doctors tend toward obsessive-compulsive traits. They help reinforce the rigorous study habits necessary to succeed in medical school and the thorough attention to detail necessary for good patient care. In this regard, Jacques was no exception. In medical school, he set aside defined hours for his studies and read each chapter in his text three times. He made sure he washed his hands between each patient and repeated his cardiac exams twice, to be sure he didn't miss any findings.

These traits had served him well in his practice, where his reputation for thoroughness contributed to the number of colleagues who referred cardiology cases to him for consultation and a loyal following of patients. However, obsessions do not serve you well when you have a child in harm's way. Returning home from the embassy, Jacques followed Omart and his squad throughout the house, peering over their shoulders as they dusted for fingerprints and watching intently as they set up their radio-direction finder and eavesdropping equipment near the cell phone charger in the kitchen. He kept asking the same questions over and over; how long would they need to wait for the next call? How could they be sure that Agnes would not be harmed? How long would it take for the fingerprints results to return? How does the radio direction finder work?

Patient by nature and sympathetic to the plight of Jacques and Rose, Omart answered these questions each time they were asked. "Usually, the kidnappers make you wait a day or two to heighten your anxiety and ramp up the pressure so that you'll deliver the ransom. There is no way of knowing if they'll harm her, but usually they don't. They just want the money. In any event, you'll need to insist she is unharmed as a condition of paying the ransom. Don't pin much hope on us finding any fingerprints – they (the kidnappers) probably wore latex gloves, and unless they've been arrested in the U.S., even if we find some, they are probably going to be worthless. The RDF triangulates with another unit we have in the embassy. When they call, you'll need to keep them on the line for a while in order to get a precise fix."

After the F.B.I. team had set up their gear, Jacques began pacing. He paced the rest of the evening and through the night, biting his nails as he paced, walking from one wall of the kitchen to the other and checking the time on the clock each time he passed it. As he paced, he ruminated. *Who could have done this... Why us? Why didn't I listen to Rose? What can I do to find her?*

His greatest obsession was his fear that Agnes would be killed. He was not sure he could live with that. In fact, he even thought of suicide, so wracked with guilt was his conscience. Yes, he might hang himself – he didn't own a pistol, and during his residency, he had seen too many botched overdoses. Then he waivered, realizing that Rose and his sons would need him, then waivered back to suicide again, torn with guilt over the thought that he might possibly have contributed to his daughter's death.

While Jacques paced, Rose sat on the sofa, leaning against

Josette, quietly sobbing. Omart and his squad took turns napping on the children's beds and standing-by at their equipment. Hours passed. With each hour, Jacques' and Rose's anticipation and anxiety increased exponentially. Omart had warned them that a long wait might be one of the kidnappers' tactics. Living that wait was a nightmare.

Chapter 11
Negotiations

Day Three
Auguste rolled off his mat, grabbed his pants and shirt off a chair next to it – the only piece of furniture in his tin shack – dressed, and stepped outside. Although the September sun had just risen, it was already oppressively hot in Cité Soleil, so close to sea-level and with so many shacks built wall-to-wall, blocking whatever feeble breeze that might attempt to penetrate it. The rains of the night before flooded the paths between the shacks with muddy-brown water. Barefoot toddlers happily splashed in it while older children in their school uniforms and adults heading for work tip-toed around the puddles' margins or hopped from plank to plank on the boards that were set down as makeshift bridges.

There was a corner market at the closest intersection, where he bought some coffee and a piece of grilled chicken for breakfast, then slogged through the slop in his bare feet – there was no need to get his new sneakers muddy, he reasoned – as he navigated the few blocks to Ogou's lair.

He found everything around him oppressive; the day's heat, the din made by the nightly rain pouring on thousands of tin roofs, the hordes of people, seemingly shoulder to shoulder, day and night, weaving in and out of the slum's streets, paths, and alleys. Two hundred thousand people trapped by poverty in an area the size of a few soccer fields. Lately, the daily misery was compounded by nightly gunfire – rival gangs settling scores – and mornings that found the streets soaked with blood. This surge in violence, a consequence of the anarchy that descended on Cité Soleil and other slums in 2005 as pro- and anti-Aristide gangs were armed in anticipation of rebellion, horrified the older, more long-term residents of Cité Soleil, poor but still imbued with traditional Haitian virtue. They hated the gangs but could do nothing to control them.

Similarly, they hated the likes of Auguste – youth who had been corrupted by power or money or drugs. They could tell by his dress and jewelry as he walked to Ogou's shack that he was one of these corrupt ones. They glared at him with undisguised scorn as he passed by.

Yes, Cité Soleil was Hell on Earth, but to give the devil his due, it had saved his life, or so Auguste thought. He had left Granthier two years before after his mother died. It only took a little asking around to latch onto Ogou. Working as his "mule," transporting drugs up to St. Marc for shipment to the U.S. earned him enough to buy some hip-hop jewelry, jeans, and sneakers and to buy food at the corner market rather than cooking it himself. He could even pay for sex on occasion, but not as often as he would like. The problem was that Ogou paid him very little – there were too many others willing to take his place; a simple matter of supply and demand, Ogou had explained.

His share of the ransom would be his ticket out. He dreamed of renting an apartment in Delmas – one with electricity four hours a day, running water, and a flushing toilet. He'd take classes to learn English, then he could get a real job as a waiter or bartender in one of the nicer hotels, perhaps even the Montana!

The miseries of Cité Soleil had stifled his conscience but

had not entirely snuffed it out.

"We aren't really going to kill her," he rationalized to himself as he weaved through the throngs that filled the alleyways. "It's really just about the money – her parents must have plenty of it, they're doctors living in America! It (the ransom) will be a drop in the bucket for them and get me out of here forever!"

Ogou had brought Auguste into the conspiracy for several reasons. Most importantly, he wanted to be invisible. In case the plan unraveled, in case the kidnappers got caught, he wanted someone else – Auguste and Wilson – to blame. He also needed someone unknown to Agnes, younger and stronger than Wilson, to remove Agnes physically from her bed and to carry her to the getaway car and later to the goat pen. Finally, he wanted someone other than himself to negotiate with Agnes' father. Having spent most of his life in Brooklyn, Ogou did not speak Kreyol well and spoke no French. His lack of language skills could complicate the negotiations and perhaps lead to his identification by the authorities who had a list of deportees with criminal records. For that reason, Auguste had placed the first ransom call the day after the kidnapping and was returning to Ogou's lair that morning. He was to call Jacques, with Ogou eavesdropping, to make sure they had raised the ransom.

Auguste wiped his muddy feet on the shag carpet as he entered Ogou's den. They fist-bumped each other, then Ogou gave Auguste his instructions; they wanted $200,000, not a *gourde* (the Haitian currency, worth about three cents) less, within three days, or Agnes would be killed.

Auguste tried not to glance at the naked young woman huddled in the corner of the room, but he could not help himself. He both admired Ogou and envied him. Ogou always had these girls in his lair – sometimes more than one. He would keep them until he tired of them, then he sold them to pimps in the Dominican Republic. He looked at her furtively as Ogou gave his instructions. He wanted her. Perhaps, when Ogou tired of her, he could buy her with some portion of the ransom, rather than shipping her to D.R.

The phone rang only once. Jacques answered immediately. "Do you have the money yet?" Auguste inquired. "If you do, we can release your princess early."

"Keep him on the phone as long as you can, so we can get a fix," whispered Omart, as he covered the cell phone's speaker with his hand.

"Well, it's been difficult," Jacques answered. "Will you take $50,000 U.S.?"

Fifty thousand U.S. dollars was a fortune to Auguste. Even his small fraction of that would be enough to get out of Cité Soleil. "I don't know, I'll have to ask my boss," Auguste stammered.

Ogou, dumbfounded that Auguste had not followed his instructions, smacked him in the face and grabbed the phone. He then did something he had hoped he wouldn't have to do. He spoke to Jacques in English. "Its $200,000 in three days or your daughter dies," he shouted, then hung up.

"Did you recognize either of the voices?" Omart asked Jacques as soon as the call ended.

"No…" Jacques responded.

"Then there's at least three of them; an insider and the two on the phone. The one who spoke English is probably a criminal deportee. Our RDF says they called from Cité Soleil, but we can't be sure exactly where – too many shacks crammed into so little space and too little time on the phone."

Chapter 12
The Cement Factory

All the way down the mountain, Michel went back and forth in his mind, trying to figure out how to rescue the girl. Their dialogue had been brief and furtive, as Agnes feared being seen in conversation by her guard. He didn't have the time, or if the truth be known, the heart to tell her he was so poor, he did not have a phone. In fact, he never had the need for one and had never even used one. Thinking about it, he knew of no one in his entire community that had one! There was a Teleco station in Croix des Bouquets, the nearest town of any significance, about six miles – two hours' walking distance. To use that station, he'd need a phone card or some *ti kob* (small change). He had neither. He thought briefly about just going to the police – there was a police station in Croix de Bouquets Center-Ville – telling Agnes' story and giving them the number written on the shard he carried with him. Then it would be their responsibility to rescue her, not his. But no, he reasoned, the police were not to be trusted. For that matter, they might not even be there! In the time since President Aristide left, many police had abandoned their posts. Those that remained, with little supervision, simply went through the motions. Security was left to the UN troops, but all they did was drive around in their Humvees. For all he knew, the police might even be in on the plot! There were stranger things happening in these strange times. No, it was his responsibility to see that the girl was rescued. *Bondye* (God) must have a reason for his path and the girl's to have crossed. He would do the best he could and put his trust in *Bondye*.

The market women ascending the path were perplexed that Michel, lost in thought, did not return their greetings. He heard his grandfather's voice in his mind, *"Never leave a stranger in distress."* His grandfather said this often, as one of the pearls of wisdom – "*parol granmoun*" or "words of the wise person" – he recited as a litany for Michel to repeat night after night. It's a paradox – Haiti is a land of paradoxes – that in a country where so few can read, everyone aspires to wisdom, and wisdom is passed down by word of mouth from generation to generation. It's not only good, but also wise to never leave a stranger in distress, for someday you might be lost and in need of help yourself! So, although only eighteen, Michel aspired to be wise like his grandparents.

Do unto others as you would have others do unto you, he thought as he descended the mountain. He prayed to his ancestors for guidance. They were his "*Ti Lwa*"; his own personal saints who knew him and would help him through this test of his faith in God's will. It was from them that the answer to his dilemma came.

Compared to its parent French, there is no verb "*avoir*" (to have) in Kreyol. Whenever we would use the word "to have," Haitians use "*genyen*" or "*gen,*" from the archaic French "to gain or earn." So, no Haitian peasant actually has anything. Everything is gained or earned. Michel would gain Agnes' freedom the same way his parents and grandparents gained anything – through hard work!

Cheri leaned over her front porch railing, anxiously awaiting Michel's silhouette to emerge from the crowded street in front of her. He had hardly ever been late before, and his supper was growing cold. Perhaps he had an accident on the mountain, she worried. Around seven thirty, she recognized his unmistakable stride coming down the street towards her. His trademark smile, usually visible even in the darkness, however, was absent. As they entered their house, he looked behind them, to be sure no one was following him.

After kissing her on both cheeks and rubbing Jean-Peter's head, he told her not to worry about his supper – he had something important to discuss. He had found a girl near one of his pens that morning, a kidnap victim. He wanted to help her, but rescuing her would be dangerous, not only for himself, but also for Cheri and Jean-Peter. He had a plan, but before he executed it, he wanted to talk to her.

As Cheri listened intently, Michel explained how he overheard the conversation with the three kidnappers, as well as his subsequent encounter with Agnes. Fearing they would kill her family if she fled, the child had voluntarily stayed behind. She gave him her father's phone number, telling him her father would know what to do. At this point, Michel showed Cheri the chard, with Agnes' father's phone number written on it.

"These are bad guys," Michel explained as he finished his story. "I heard them talking. They'll kill her if her family doesn't pay the ransom, or if we don't find a way to set her free. She wouldn't come back with me, fearing they would carry out their threat against her family, or find her here with us. She's light-skinned, Cheri, so she'd be easy to find here in Lamardelle, and one of the kidnappers seems to be a *kay-moun* (a home-boy, i.e., a resident of Granthier) – he could easily find out who my pen belongs to…"

Without hesitating, Cheri responded that of course, Michel must help rescue her – it was clear that *Bondye* (God) and the *Lwa* (Vodou saints) had chosen him. It was the right thing to do and the *Lwa* would protect her, him, and his family. Just to be safe, however, she would take herself and Jean-Peter to her mother's house, several blocks away, for the next few days.

"How do you plan to call the girl's father?" she inquired. Not only did they not have a phone, but none of their neighbors had phones. To make matters worse, they had no *ti kob* (spare change) on hand to buy a phone card – Cheri had gone to the market that day to buy food and Jean-Peter's first set of shoes. The goat that they planned to sell that month was sick and needed to be nursed back to health before it could be sold. The only savings they had was a small amount they had put aside for Jean-Peter's school. They had both vowed, however, that those funds would never be spent on anything else but Jean-Peter's education. Michel always felt badly that his own parents couldn't afford to send him to school and was committed to see that his own child would be educated. To be sure it was safe, Cheri had buried it in a small box behind the house.

Michel then disclosed his plan, worked through in his mind towards the end of his descent from the mountain. Tomorrow he would go to one of the cement-block makers in Croix de Bouquets and make enough blocks to earn money for a phone call. He'd call Agnes' father from the Teleco station and be done with it – one day to do the right thing and they'd both sleep well at night.

"What about the goats?" Cheri inquired.

"They'll be fine for one day," Michel responded. "Before I left, I loaded the pen with extra grass and thistles."

In contrast to rural Haiti, where homes are built from wood, homes in Port-au-Prince and its suburbs are built almost exclusively from "home-made" concrete blocks. Homes – both legitimate and those of squatters – have been built over decades. As the owners earn a little "*ti-kob,*" they add on to their edifice block by block. Concrete blocks, therefore, are in constant demand. The raw materials – sand and limestone – are abundant in Haiti, and all one needs are a few wooden molds and some laborers to set up a concrete block factory.

Early the next morning, Michel rose before dawn and briskly walked to the largest block factory in Croix-de-Bouquets and explained his need for *ti-kob* to the *proprieteur*. Toussaint, the proprietor, was a kindly old gentleman, but also a businessman. Through the years, he used his cement blocks factory as a microfinance bank for those members of the community in need. Michel's grandfather and father had gone to him in hard times – in fact, Michel and his father had made blocks to purchase his initial set of goats. These prior dealings gave Michel the cachet to stride to the head of the line, past the other day-labor hopefuls to speak directly to Toussaint.

After exchanging greetings and mutual salutes showing respect and honor, Michel told his story. It was quickly agreed that he could earn one *gourde* for every block he produced. It would take 250 *gourdes* to buy fifteen minutes of time on Teleco, the public phone system. Therefore, Michel would need to make 250 concrete blocks to make the hopefully life-saving phone call.

By eight o'clock, Michel was working, shirt off, sweating,

shoveling limestone and sand into a large cauldron, adding water, and stirring the mixture with a wooden plank. He then scooped the wet concrete out with his hands and filled a series of molds, levelling them off with another board. By noon, he had laid out enough blocks to dry in the sun to earn enough for the Teleco phone call. At one thirty, the sky clouded over. He hadn't factored in the possibility of afternoon rain, which would ruin the half-set block-molds that had already started to set. Looking skyward, he prayed to Bondye and asked his grandfather to intercede on his behalf. By two, the clouds thinned over Croix de Bouquet, even as torrents of rain fell on Morne Kenskoff. By three, the blocks were set. Michel proudly showed his handiwork to Toussaint, who paid him in cash – just enough for one call.

Chapter 13
Mambo

Soon after Michel left for the factory, Cheri grabbed a large spoon, went out to the back of their home and dug up the box that contained their savings. She took out three hundred gourdes, then planted the box back in the ground, carefully manicuring the surface of the hole so that no one would notice it had been disturbed. She then returned to her home, washed the spoon, hoisted Jean Pierre on her hip, and hiked the few hundred yards to her mother's home.

"I need to leave Jean Pierre with you for a little bit," she told her mother. "I'm going to visit Mambo Maryse." She then recounted the story Michel had shared with her the night before. "I couldn't sleep last night, *Mami.* I know Michel is doing the right thing, but it's dangerous! I prayed to *Erzilie* all night. You should pray also – pray for Michel and pray for that poor girl."

Mambo Maryse's home looked like all the others in the neighborhood, except it was painted black and red rather than the customary blue and white. Black and red were Vodou colors – black for the people and red for the blood their ancestors shed to set them free. Inside, however, the walls had been gutted to create a *hougan*, a Vodou Temple. In the center was a thick wooden pole, the *poto mitan,* the biblical Tree of Life. The walls were decorated with pictures of saints and in each corner were banks of votive candles and appliquéd jars filled with potions. Mambo Maryse, dressed in red and black, with her head covered with a red shawl, embraced Cheri and kissed her on both cheeks.

"What brings you here so early in the morning?"

Cheri handed her the three hundred gourdes she had resurrected in the morning darkness.

"An offering," she whispered. "My husband needs your prayers."

Mambo Maryse listened intently as Cheri recounted the story of Michel's discovery of the child and his plan to rescue her. She asked no questions, but instead, sent her older daughter to fetch her younger sister. "Put on your white dresses," she advised. "I'll need you to serve as acolytes. Bring your brother, also, with his *tambour* (drum)."

While waiting for her children to return, Maryse took a tool out of a box of chalk powder and used it to draw a *veve* on the floor of the *hougan* – symbolic representations of Vodou spirits. First, she drew a large serpentine semi-circle in front of the *poto mitan* – a pole in the center of the hougan that represents the tree of life. "This is *Danballah* (the serpent)," she explained. "He will protect your husband." Next, at the base of the serpent, she drew a heart with a cross at the base. "This is *Erzilie*. We will call on her to save the child."

Vodou is a fusion of Roman Catholicism and ancient African Animism. It's an interesting marriage. If Catholicism views the spiritual realm as abstract and immaterial, Vodou sees it as palpably real. If Catholic ritual is dry and rote, Vodou is vibrant theatre. There's an expression in Kreyol – a prayer that's sung is twice the prayer; a prayer that's sung and danced is thrice the prayer.

Big boned, with wide hips and large breasts, Maryse and her two acolytes began their dance and chants slowly, rhythmically, with Maryse singing a litany of invocations to Erzilie, the protectress of women and children, followed by a response, "May it be God's will" from the two acolytes. As the rhythm of the drum beat slowly increased, so did the intensity of the singing and the whirling of the dance.

It was a sensual, hypnotic, almost sexual dance, a *calenda*, the dance, in Haitian folklore, that launched the Haitian Revolution – a dance for freedom, a dance Maryse prayed would set Agnes free. It climaxed with a *criz* – Maryse, collapsing to the floor, possessed by the spirit of Erzilie, herself dead, but living through Erzilie, she spoke in a voice not her own, "Go now, Cheri, with peace in your heart. God will bless your husband and this child!"

Chapter 14
Contact

The Teleco building in Croix-de-Bouquets was painted the same blue and white colors as the police station in Petionville. Michel waited in line until his turn came, then handed the operator the note with the charcoal-written number of Agnes' father's cell phone on the back.

"*Eske ou ka rele numero sa pou mwen?* (Can you call this number for me?)" he asked. It was a code to the operator, letting him know that Michel couldn't read numbers and had rarely used a Teleco phone before. At the same time, he slipped his money through the cashier's window

"*Biensur, monsieur,*" the operator responded politely. It was routine that the caller might need his assistance. "*Ale a numero kat.* (Go to booth number four)."

Booth 4 was fully enclosed, almost like a confessional, except for the small window in the door. Michel sat there for a few minutes, not knowing what to expect, when the phone rang; a loud, startling, brilliant ring. Michel picked up the receiver.

"*Yon moment,*" said the operator.

The phone did not even finish ringing once before Jacques answered it. He had been sitting beside it all day, waiting for his brother in Brooklyn to call about raising the ransom, hoping the embassy would call saying Agnes had been found, fearing the kidnappers would call, upping the ante. What he was not prepared for was the voice of Michel on the other end of the phone. "*Bonswa, Monsieur,*" Michel began. "Do you have a daughter named Agnes?"

"Yes..." responded Jacques cautiously, wondering if the caller was one of the kidnappers or perhaps an imposter – a *charlatan* – someone who had heard about the kidnapping by word-of-mouth and was trying to cash in. Omart, at his side, along with his translator, Mathieu, noted that their caller ID had already identified the location of the call – "Croix-de-Bouquets Teleco".

"She gave me this number and asked me to call you. She said you'd figure out how to rescue her. She's in a goat pen high up on Kenskoff Mountain." Michel hoped that this would be all the information Agnes' father would need, that he could now say good-bye, return home to Cheri and Jean-Peter, his commitment to Agnes fulfilled.

Jacques, however, with prompting from Omart, had a different plan. "I need to ask you a few questions to make sure you're not a *charlatan*. First, what is your name?"

"Michel Jean-Baptiste, *monsieur.*"

"What do you do?"

"I herd goats. That's why I found her – they hid her in my goat pen!"

"Why didn't you take her with you when you found her?"

"I tried to take her, but she refused to come with me. They threatened to kill her if she tried to escape, and you and your family also. She didn't know if they would come back. Besides, she'd like you to catch these guys. She said you'd figure out a way to set her free and catch these guys."

"What was she wearing?"

"A yellow nightgown..."

"Can you lead us to her?"

"Sure. I go up the mountain every day."

"Stay where you are, a police rescue squad will rendezvous with you within the hour."

Michel hesitated for a moment. Part of him wanted to run away – he didn't trust the police. How did he know they hadn't been bribed by the kidnappers? If so, what would stop them from throwing him in jail and declaring the crime solved? He had heard rumors to that effect with some of the previous kidnappings. The kidnappers themselves posed an even greater threat to him and his family – if they were willing to kill Agnes and her family, they would be just as willing to kill his, particularly if they eluded capture.

"Are you still there?" Jacques grew more anxious with every passing second of silence.

"Yes, I'm here." In his mind, Michel heard the voice of his grandfather: *Never leave a stranger in distress*. "Okay. I'll be here, waiting for them."

"They'll be *blan* (whites), because I'm a U.S. citizen and their shirts will have the letters F-B-I on them." Jacques volunteered, hoping to both ease Michel's anxiety about the local police and help him identify them when they arrived. Michel was too embarrassed to tell him that he didn't know how to read.

Jacques thanked Michel for his courage and said good-bye. Omart immediately dialed the embassy. The officer of the day patched him through to his unit. "Scramble! We're heading out to the Teleco station in Croix-de-Bouquet," he stammered excitedly. "We just got a call from someone there who claims he knows where the child is – somewhere up Kenskoff Mountain. He's a goatherd or a shepherd or something like that."

Chapter 15
Despair

Omart and his Special Operations Unit weaved through the traffic between the Montana Hotel and the Croix-de-Bouquets Teleco, exhorting their driver to go as quickly as possible. Omart was worried his informant would get cold feet. After all, what was in it for him? After a shortcut through Museau, then down Rue Delmas, they navigated the chaos of Port-au-Prince's streets, across Avenue Haile Selassie to the airport road, weaving in and out of traffic. Things bogged down in gridlock at the main square in Croix-de-Bouquets – a staging area for trucks and *tap-taps* heading into the countryside – so a few blocks from the Teleco, Omart decided to get out with his interpreter and walk the rest of the way. In addition to the small window of opportunity to hopefully rescue the kidnapped child, there was the added benefit of having something meaningful to do, after a month of identifying dead bodies, filing reports, and watching from the sidelines as the rebellion against President Aristide unfolded.

Michel, who decided to wait under a tree about fifty yards away from the Teleco office, stepped out of the darkness as the two men passed him; one Black, one White, each with three letters on their jerseys then strode alongside them.

"*Blan! Eske-w poliz? (*Stranger, are you police?*)*" he asked Omart. It was a safe bet these were the guys he was looking for – one rarely saw a white person walking the streets of Croix de Bouquets.

"*Oui, Poliz American,*" responded Mathieu, the interpreter. "*Biwo Fedwal Investigatyon.*"

"Hi, I'm Omart," said Omart with a muscular handshake. "Mathieu, tell him to come with us. We'll talk in our car."

Omart took to Michel right away, even though he could not talk to him directly. He liked the firmness of his grip and the fact that as he shook his hand, he also beat his chest with his left hand in a traditional Haitian salute. He was impressed with his wiry frame and purposeful stride. In another life, he would have made a good special agent, he thought. Most of all, he liked his smile. Michel was always smiling, even when Omart explained the possible peril he might be facing.

After telling Omart and his squad a little about himself and his family, Michel recounted in considerable detail the conversation he overheard among the kidnappers and his encounter with Agnes.

"As I suspected, one of them is on the inside," Omart said to his team. He then peppered Michel about the appearance of the kidnappers.

They had no distinguishing features, Michel related, other than their jewelry and fancy clothes, which had impressed him.

"That doesn't help us much," responded Omart, chuckling at Michel's lack of sophistication. "Every punk gang leader and drug dealer in Cité Soleil dresses that way. We'll have to draw them out in the open, get them to go back to your goat pen. Can you take us there?"

"Sure, as soon as it's light enough to see the trail," Michel volunteered enthusiastically.

"Good, that gives us just enough time to hatch a plan. We'll have to take you with us to our hotel and your family too – it's safer for all of you while you show us the way to the goat-pen."

Chapter 16
Culture Shock

Omart was growing impatient. What he thought would be a five-minute wait outside Michel's mother-in-law's house had grown to an hour. They had already lost forty-five precious minutes driving Michel back to Lamardelle. Maybe his first impressions were wrong. Maybe he had second thoughts and had given them the slip. There was no way they could ever find him again if he chose to run away – this was a part of Haiti he never knew existed. Finally, Michel returned with Cheri and Jean-Peter, proudly introducing them to Omart and his unit.

"What took so long?" Omart asked, somewhat irritated, through the interpreter.

"Well, my wife's mother had prepared me dinner," Michel responded innocently. "I had to eat it – we can't waste food, you know. Besides, yesterday I gave my lunch to the girl and had no breakfast this morning. I was hungry!"

On the ride to the hotel, Omart asked Michel why he had waited a day to call Agnes' father. They only had two days left, after all, and they were coming down to the wire. Michel's response – a matter-of-fact recounting of his cement-block making to buy a phone card – shocked Omart to his core. He had seen Haiti's poverty as he cruised Port-au-Prince's streets through the window of his Humvee. Never, until that moment, however, did he truly comprehend that there were people in this world too poor to make a phone call. Nor did he realize that someone as impoverished as he now realized Michel was would nevertheless risk his own life to rescue a stranger. In an instant, Omart's affection for Michel matured into a deep admiration. *That's hopefully one lucky little girl. This kind of hero would never surface in Miami,* he mused.

The gulf between Michel's world and Omart's world was poignantly exposed at the hotel. Michel and Cheri were awestruck by its size, the brilliance of its illumination, and the elegance of the guests gathered around the bar and the pool terrace.

Cheri resisted the bellman's attempt to take the small sack of clothes she had brought with her until Mathieu explained that it was customary for the bellman to take a guest's bags to the room when they checked in. Their room was actually larger than their house in Croix-de-Bouquet, and full of amenities – air conditioning, television, showers, sinks and toilets – things that they had never seen or used before. The bellman only turned on the TV and air conditioner, leaving it to Omart and Mathieu to explain the use of the various other fixtures in the bathroom.

Omart wrote the number of his room on a piece of paper and showed Michel how to press the same numbers on his phone. "Call me if you need anything," he said, and then retired to his room to call Agnes' father.

"Well, this goatherd seems to be the real deal," he told him. "He seems a little bit like he's from another world – very rustic – but he knows exactly where your daughter is, and there's a good chance that if we play our cards right, we can not only get your daughter back, but catch the guys who did this. Now, here's what I want you to do…"

Chapter 17
The Trap

Day Four
"Let it ring!" bellowed Ogou to Clarisse. "I'll choose to call them back if I want to."

Clarisse, only a few years older than Agnes, cowered whenever Ogou shouted like that – Ogou was frightening enough when he was merely sneering at her, threatening to send her off to some pimp in the D.R. By answering his phones, bringing him a beer when he demanded it, and making him dinner, she could pretend for her family and their neighbors that she was simply his housekeeper. No one else, however, in Cité Soleil had a housekeeper tidying things up in the nude.

"Sugar, can I put some clothes on before Auguste gets here? He makes me nervous when he stares at me…"

"Sure, if you want. Just bring me the phone first," answered Ogou, mildly annoyed that Clarisse cared at all what Auguste thought, particularly since he had bungled the initial negotiations. There was no way, even when he tired of her, that he would ever let Auguste have her.

Today was the day that his scheme for riches would reach fruition. He had researched it thoroughly; his victim was carefully chosen, and his accomplices were all held on a short leash. He was sure that Agnes' parents would deliver the ransom in full.

With the money Ogou made off drugs, he paid off four contiguous squatters in Cité Soleil to move out and built himself a "headquarters." He decorated the interior of the cardboard and tin shacks with a garish collection of "Kitch Kreyol" – shag carpets, second-hand sofas and ersatz tiffany lamps, powered by his *delco* battery bank and surreptitious tap-in to the powerline that supplied Ste. Catherine's hospital, about a hundred yards away.

He had parlayed his drug connections (and the money it brought) into a certain status in Cité Soleil. He had his sex slaves (Clarisse was only one of many) and his jewelry and entourage. He could see, however, the handwriting on the wall. The upcoming elections would ultimately cancel out the anarchy he depended on for his drug money. That's why kidnapping Agnes was so important. After paying off Wilson, Plato, and Auguste, he'd have plenty left over. He'd be able to set himself up in comfort forever – perhaps a brothel, perhaps a lotto operation. The details mattered little – with a hundred thousand dollars in his pocket, he could be king of Cité Soleil.

Clarisse brought the cell phone to him and Ogou stared at the number on the "missed call" page. Sure enough, it was Agnes' father's cell-phone number.

Well, I've made him sweat enough, he thought. *It's time to turn his fear into some cold, hard cash.* He hit the redial button.

"So, it's Day Four." He spoke in English, not even attempting Kreyol, since Auguste had already blown his cover. "Do you have the ransom, or do I have to kill your little 'ho'?"

Jacques restrained his anger and channeled it towards vengeance. "Yes, we've raised the ransom, but as it turns out, several people have called saying they have my daughter.

There's lots of *charlatans* out there. How do I know that you are the one?"

"Well," Ogou responded nonchalantly, "would you like her nightgown, her panties, or both? She'll be fine running around naked like all the other poor kids!"

Omart grabbed Jacques' arm and whispered, "Don't lose it. Keep him talking so we can more precisely locate him."

Jacques bristled but managed to restrain himself. "You do that and the deal is off. I'd rather see my daughter dead than humiliated. Besides, I need some assurance she's still alive. I want a note in her handwriting, dated today, stating she's alive. Either that or you can have her call me on this phone."

Ogou was taken aback by the resolve in Jacques' voice. Perhaps he had overplayed his hand. He saw through immediately the phone call trick – clearly Jacques had gone to the authorities and were hoping to identify the place they were hiding Agnes by triangulating on his cell-phone transmission. For all he knew, they could be getting a fix on him now. He needed to act quickly. Yes, the signed note was the better option.

"Okay, I'll have that note to you by tomorrow!" and he hung up.

Chapter 18
Plato's Dilemma

On the morning of her fourth day in captivity, Agnes was awakened by the bleating of the goats. Cold and damp and still thirsty, she considered licking the rain and condensation off the slats, as the goats were doing, for after that first taste, she dared not drink the water her kidnappers left her. Shortly after sunrise, however, she heard Plato approaching. He said little as he forced two more plastic bags of water through the slats and a small tin of porridge under the gate.

"You'll be no good to us dead," he murmured, "so you better eat and drink these," he said, as he turned to walk away.

Agnes took some solace in that terse comment – at least she had another day.

As the sun rose higher and higher in the sky, the day heated up and thirst gnawed more and more in her stomach. A dark thought gnawed on her mind: tomorrow could be the last day of her life. Against her own will, she opened the packets of water with her teeth and gulped down their contents, then scooped out the contents of the tin with her fingers.

Plato saw no sense in sitting with Agnes, as she refused to talk to him. He dared not release her to play with the other children a second time – this time, she might be desperate enough to run away. Better, he thought to sit up on his porch and scan the horizon for the goatherd. He hoped he wouldn't appear again, but if he did, he'd have to intercept him and kill him. When Ogou first told him he might have to do something like that, he thought he was joking. After the threats Ogou made to both him and Agnes, he now knew that Ogou was serious. If he did not kill Michel, Ogou would kill him.

Agnes also spent the day looking futilely for Michel, praying for his appearance or some sign of impending deliverance. As she prayed, she paced the five steps it took to traverse from one side of the pen to the other, scattering any goats that got in her way. Morning passed into afternoon and finally evening. With evening came exhaustion and despair.

Shortly after lapsing into a fitful sleep, Agnes was awakened by an intense urge to vomit. She resisted this urge for as long as she could, sitting in the darkness, leaning forward, shifting her weight to her arms to take pressure off her stomach wall. Alas, her stomach's need to empty its contents was not to be denied. When she finally vomited, it was so forceful and voluminous that the foul and acid stomach contents came out her nose as well as her mouth. She couldn't help but aspirate some of it, which provoked a violent coughing fit. Two more times she vomited, followed by "dry heaves." Shortly thereafter, her stomach started cramping. Soon, diarrhea spilled out of her like water from a bathtub spigot. It smelled so foul that even the goats avoided being near it – fleeing "en masse" to the farthest corner of the pen.

Plato sensed something was amiss at dawn's first light. On the other mornings since Agnes' capture, he watched her silhouette pace within the pen. This morning, he only saw the silhouette of the goats mulling about. Had she run away? Rather than preparing her meal, as he had done on the prior mornings, he bolted out the door and ran down the hill to the pen.

As he drew near the pen, his relief to see Agnes still imprisoned inside was muted by the fact that she was clearly quite ill – lying listlessly on the floor of the pen in her own diarrhea. The smell of vomit and diarrhea was so offensive he reflexively turned away. He then forced himself to unlatch the pen and pull Agnes out.

Her several bouts of diarrhea through the night left her too weak to stand. She was shivering and coughing and sobbing, although she was too dehydrated to produce tears. Plato touched her forehead. She was burning with fever. Plato was on the verge of panic. Ogou, Auguste, and Wilson would be coming in a few hours. If they found her like this, they would beat him severely. If she died, they'd probably kill him.

He ran up to his home, picked up two buckets, a towel, and a rag and headed to the one functioning well located in the center of Granthier. He quickly filled the two buckets with water, lifted one atop his head, and then raced back to the goat pen. The round trip consumed a precious half-hour. Agnes, delirious, was talking incoherently – something about a goatherd who had failed her. Plato took off her nightie, rinsed it in one bucket of water, rung it out and placed it on the side of the pen facing the sun to dry. He then used the rag and the one remaining bucket of clean water to wash her from head to toe – first her face, then her front. To wash her back, he lifted her limp body and slung her over his left shoulder, holding her there with his left arm while washing her with his right hand. The coldness of the water, enhanced by the freshening morning breeze, roused Agnes from her delirium. As some semblance of consciousness returned, however, she was startled to discover herself in the seeming embrace of a youth who claimed he wanted to be her friend but whom she knew could not be trusted. Fearing the worst, she attempted to scream, but only a groan came out, followed by a coughing fit. Gathering her remaining strength, she struggled to free herself from Plato's grasp, pummeled his face with her fists and attempted to poke her finger in his left eye socket.

"No, no, no!" exclaimed Plato. "It's not what you think! You're sick! I found you covered with crap and your clothes all soiled. They're coming today, and if it all goes well, perhaps they'll set you free. But you wouldn't want them to see you the way I found you this morning."

Agnes didn't believe a word of it and continued to flail at him. Her strength, however, was spent, and her mind in a fog. Exhausted, she slumped back over his shoulder.

Stung that Agnes would even think that he would assault her, Plato carried her to a nearby rocky ledge – he didn't want to lay her now clean body back on the grass and dirt. He gently rolled her off his shoulder and averted his eyes, covering her with his towel.

By the position of the sun, Plato reckoned it was about nine o'clock. Wilson and Auguste would be there soon. It was too late to think about carrying her to a clinic – the nearest clinic was in Kenskoff village, a two-hour hike, not to mention the consequences he might face if the conspirators arrived to find them gone. He decided he'd need to get some water into her, quickly, even if it required something akin to water boarding!

He ran to the bucket with the fresher water, grabbed it and a rag and returned to Agnes' side. He forced her jaw open by cupping one hand around her chin and pressing her cheeks on either side with his thumb and forefinger. He soaked the rag with water from the bucket, held it over her mouth and squeezed. He cradled Agnes' head in his lap and began squeezing water from the rag into Agnes' open mouth.

The stream of water in the back of her throat roused Agnes again from her stupor. She reflexively swallowed a few gulps then clenched her teeth and sealed her lips. "No!" she rasped.

"Please drink some water I've brought you from the village well. It's good water. Otherwise, you might die!" Plato implored.

Indeed, Agnes knew she was dying. Her strength was gone. Nausea and fever made it difficult to think and she was short of breath. She was dry as sand and intensely thirsty. She was not, however, going to drink any water.

"If God wants me to die, then I'll die!" Agnes struggled to get these words out of her parched throat. "If I'm gone, then my parents won't need to pay my ransom and my family won't be killed!"

"I'll be killed!" Plato exclaimed. "Please drink some more of this water!"

The more Plato exhorted her to drink, the more Agnes resisted. She should never have given in to the urge to drink the water and eat the food he brought her yesterday, she thought. Her thirst was overwhelming, but her ability to say "no" was her last vestige of freedom. It was the only thing she could still control.

Frustrated, Plato poured the two buckets of water over the mess in the center of the goat pen. He made two more trips to the well in the center of Granthier, using three buckets to further wash out the pen and saving one for Agnes in case she changed her mind. "Here, your clothes are dry now. Dress yourself! They'll be here soon. You don't want them to see you naked. They're not as kind as me…"

After a half hour, the sun had dried the floor of the pen. Plato decided that if Agnes died, he best not be with her. He even thought briefly about running away, so intensely did he fear the violence that would be inflicted upon him if she perished, but he realized that by abandoning her he would forfeit any hope of the *"ti cob"* Auguste had promised him. Instead, he decided to return home. If he were in his house, he could plead ignorance. He therefore carried her back to the pen, laying her down in a relatively clean spot and latched the gate as he left. As he ascended the path toward his home, he prayed to *Baron Samedi*, the Vodou *Lwa* of the underworld. "Please don't take her yet – you'll only have to come back for me after Wilson and Auguste find her!"

Chapter 19
Liberation

Day Five

Michel rose at four, as was his custom, dressed and kissed Cheri and Jean-Peter goodbye. He paced around the lobby of the Montana, making small talk with the night clerk and night watchman until Omart arrived at five thirty. Omart had arranged for breakfast for his team – omelets, pancakes, and French toast, which they wolfed down so that they could meet their departure deadline at six.

Michel had never seen such an abundance of food. He asked Omart if he could bring their leftovers with them. Omart looked at him quizzically.

"It's for my goats," Michel explained. "They'll be hungry! I neglected them the last two days." By the time they departed, there was a hefty bag of *fatra* in the back of their SUV.

Little did Agnes know, as the sun rose on her fifth day of captivity in the goat-pen, that a rescue team was assembling at the base of the mountain. Diarrhea and pneumonia had set in the night before, bringing her near death. She lapsed in and out of consciousness. Even when she was awake, it was difficult to focus her thoughts. If only she had run away when she had the chance, she thought. It had been three days since she had confided in the goatherd. She had expected him back that evening, but he had not returned. She had made a choice to stay rather than run to protect her family. Now, however, she was growing weaker by the hour. How foolish she had been to put her faith in a total stranger.

Under protocol, Omart scrambled a squad of Haitian National Police to make the actual arrest – his own squad had been carefully instructed that, whenever possible, Haitian sovereignty should be respected. There could be, after all, dire consequences if Americans used lethal force on Haitians – consequences ranging from a diplomatic crisis to collateral damage to innocent bystanders, to riots if the people felt the action was unjustified. The entourage therefore now consisted of the six members of Omart's squad, six Haitian police, and Michel, plus two drivers. Two squad members would stay with the Humvees while four agents, the Haitian squad plus Michel would attempt the rescue.

As the two squads strapped on their body armor and their weapons at the trail head, Michel greeted his acquaintances descending the trail, pretending he didn't know either the *blans* or the *poliz* organizing themselves behind their SUVs. It would not be like him to just stand there at the trailhead, so he would ascend a few yards with his sack of *fatra* then pretend to rest, explaining to concerned passersby that he had been ill and therefore not his usual energetic self. It took quite a while for the two units to gear up – weapons belts, body armor ,and teargas canisters. Each F.B.I. agent carried a Glock pistol and extra rounds of ammunition. The Haitian squad also donned body armor. Instead of pistols, however, each carried an M-1 rifle, on loan from the F.B.I.

At Omart's signal, Michel began his ascent, always staying in the line of sight but far enough ahead of the team so that he could deny knowledge of those that were following him. Up the mountain Michel bounded, not realizing that the weight of their armor might slow down Omart and his teams. After fifteen minutes, Omart signaled Michel to slow down so that he could narrow the gap between his guide and his teams.

Omart pushed his teams to ascend as quickly as possible. They had to move quickly – if the kidnappers got to Agnes first, they'd miss their chance. Weighted down with body armor, weapons, and gear, however, it was difficult for them to keep up with Michel. All F.B.I. agents need to pass annual "fit for duty" physicals. There had been years in the past when Omart had complained about them, calling them a bureaucratic nuisance and a waste of his time. As he and his team labored to keep up with Michel, however, he vowed never to complain about "fit for duty" regulations again. Both the F.B.I. and the Haitian squad stopped several times during the climb, breathless, shedding body armor by the side of the trail as they ascended.

When Michel stopped climbing, the squad realized they were getting close. Following Omart's hand signals, the Haitian police took up positions perpendicular to the trail, using the cover of the same spot Michel had used to eavesdrop on the kidnappers on the first day, triangulating to cover every angle. Omart caught his breath and rolled over on his back, next to Michel and Mathieu, his translator, staring first at the sky and then at the sweeping panorama beneath him. Several hours passed.

Sometime after noon, Michel nudged Omart. Two figures, one with jewelry glinting in the sunlight, were descending the trail from the summit. "It's them," Michel whispered to the translator. Omart resisted the urge to draw his pistol – F.B.I. agents are trained to draw only when they intend to shoot and to shoot only when they intend to kill. Yes, part of him wanted to just take these two out and be done with it – clearly, they had committed a heinous crime. The world would be a better place without them and, if brought to trial, there was always the possibility that some crafty lawyer would get them off. But no, Omart knew the difference between vengeance and justice, and justice would only be served if these two were arrested by their own police, remanded to the United States, and convicted by a jury there. Besides, there was still at least one more conspirator to be captured, and only these two could lead them to him.

Wilson and Auguste groused at each other as they descended toward the goat pen. This was the day they were supposed to become rich, at least by Haitian standards. Instead, Ogou had sent them down the mountain again, insisting they return with a piece of paper with the girl's handwriting on it.

The approach of two men caused the goats to stir. Wilson sat down just below the ridge, not wanting to be seen, while Auguste proceeded towards Agnes menacingly. The bleating goats, stampeding to the far side of the pen, trampled over Agnes, rousing her from her stupor.

This could be it, she thought as her mind suddenly cleared. *They could be here to kill me!* Her heart pounded and she broke out into a cold sweat. She willed away an almost overwhelming urge to purge her intestinal contents one more time – she was determined not to humiliate herself in front of her captors. She was somewhat surprised and relieved, therefore, when her captor sat down outside the pen, pulled out a notepad and pen, and insisted she write a note and sign it, declaring she was all right.

"I'm not all right!" Agnes rasped with all her remaining strength. "I'm tired of sleeping with goats, I'm hungry, thirsty, and dirty and need clean water and a real toilet! I've got a fever, probably pneumonia. I'll die soon if you don't get me out of here!"

"Great!" exclaimed Auguste in mock sympathy. "Just sign this note and in a few hours you'll be free."

Auguste could see how ill Agnes was, but he didn't care. Once they had a note in her handwriting, the ransom would be paid. Whether she survived or not was inconsequential. "Sign the note or I'll have to beat you!"

The threat of a beating had no effect on her. Her body and her mind were numb. Yet, even in her confused, delirious state, she realized the significance of the note they were asking her to sign. Perhaps her father had raised her ransom, perhaps it was true; give them what they wanted and her ordeal would be over in a matter of hours.

The goats, having not been out of their pen in two days, bleated and circled in the pen, some raising themselves up on their hind legs and pressing on the gate. For a moment, Agnes resisted Auguste's order as an act of defiance. She had resigned herself to death earlier that morning. In the end, however, she signed it. Plato was right. This man was not as kind as him. He might not stop with just a beating.

Omart withheld his signal for the Haitian police to execute the arrest as Auguste thrust the notepad through the slats in the pen. Omart wanted Agnes' signature on the note – it would be a powerful piece of evidence in court – but the wait, as Agnes initially resisted, seemed an eternity. For their part, the Haitian police had their fingers pressed slightly on the triggers of their M-1's with Auguste's back in their sights, instructed to shoot only if Agnes' life seemed in danger.

The Haitian squad leader peered intently at the pen, through his scope, patiently waiting while Agnes deliberated. When Agnes finally signed her name to the paper, he rose and yelled in Kreyol. "Stop! You are under arrest. Raise your arms and lie on the ground or you'll be shot!"

Stunned, Auguste dove face down on the ground. Wilson, however, bolted up the mountain trail, only to run into the arms of the two other Haitian police who had circled behind him. They threw him to the ground. One stood on his neck while the other handcuffed him.

Omart signaled Michel that the Haitian police had the two kidnappers under arrest. Michel approached the pen. After spreading out his *fatra*, he opened the gate. The goats rushed out, eagerly consuming the hotel breakfast leftovers. Agnes, weak and not sure her ordeal was over, lay prostrate in the center of the pen. Michel entered, smiled, and kissed her, Haitian style, on both cheeks. He had kept his promise. His grandfather, he was sure, was smiling on him. He then picked her up and carried her to the place where the squad and their prisoners were assembling. He held her in his arms while the agents encouraged her to take sips of water from their canteens.

As the fog of her delirium started to lift, Agnes struggled to sift through what had happened over the past five days – was it a nightmare? As consciousness returned, she first had trouble not only focusing, but recognizing what she saw. After a few confused minutes, she identified the smiling face looking down at her. It was the goatherd! With that, it all flooded back; the terror, the voices, the injection, the goats, the youth who wanted to be her friend but forced water down her throat. It took some time to get the words out, but finally she rasped, “I gave up on you… I thought you’d be back that night!”

“Well, I didn’t have a phone or any money, so I had to make cement blocks so I could call your father…” Michel felt compelled to tell the whole story, even though Agnes could barely make sense out of it.

“Sorry to interrupt,” Omart interjected, “but is there anyone else?

“Yes,” Agnes mumbled. “A boy – I think he lives up there,” as she pointed up to the mountain to Plato’s home.

The sound of Omart’s voice, in English, further roused Agnes’ consciousness. She stared at both captors and rescuers, trying to sort them out. One of the hand-cuffed men had his back turned away from her and his head slumped forward, trying to conceal his face. But there was no mistaking the bald spot on the back of his head. Now she recalled the vaguely familiar voice she heard on the night of the kidnapping. It was Wilson!

Chapter 20
Plato's Paralysis

Plato sat on his porch sobbing uncontrollably. He knew it was wrong to leave Agnes, but he feared what Auguste and Wilson would do to him if they came and found her dead. So, he prayed to every saint and *Lwa* he could think of to spare her life, promising to become an acolyte to Granthier's *Bokar* (Vodou Priest) if only she would survive. From his porch, he stared incessantly at the goat pen, looking for some twitch or restless movement that would signal that she was still alive.

On the night that they had left Agnes in the pen, Wilson had left Jacques' wallet and a pair of sneakers with Plato as a down payment for his services. Once again, Plato contemplated running away, this time with the sneakers. He could slip down the mountain, sell the sneakers, and probably have enough *"ti cob"* to survive for a few weeks.

He was ashamed, however, and embarrassed that he had ever gotten involved in this whole sordid affair. "Never leave a stranger in distress," his grandmother had taught him, and he had ignored her words of wisdom. He decided, therefore, to just sit there and see how things played out. What was *Bondye's* plan for him and this child?

He took some comfort that Agnes did, indeed, occasionally turn and move. He concocted a tale he would tell Auguste and Wilson as to how she had deteriorated drastically overnight and how he was awaiting their arrival to decide what to do. He noticed Auguste and Wilson arriving in the stolen SUV and walking down the path to the pen. He waved nonchalantly, hoping to buy time by pretending, as far as he knew, everything was according to plan. Let them discover her near death. He could feign ignorance. Hopefully, they'd decide to take her to a clinic, hospital, or doctor. If they did that, he'd be done with this and would head down to Cité Soleil, lesson learned, dissolve among the masses, never to get involved with evil again.

Therefore, as Wilson and Auguste descended from the road, he sat there expecting they would soon be coming for him. He wanted to take advantage of the time it would take them to descend and re-ascend to flee – there was no doubt they would brutalize him for failing to safe-guard their prize – but paralysis was slowly descending upon him.

As it turned out, he was not prepared for what actually transpired. Auguste and Wilson descended towards the pen. Then, suddenly, voices rang out, calling them to surrender. He recognized the goatherd who headed towards the pen. Yes, the goatherd – Plato knew of the goatherd and thought of warning the other accomplices about him. It was simple – if there were goats in the pen, there had to be a goatherd, and he had seen him from his porch tending to the needs of his goats every few days. Not living in Granthier to observe the goat herder's day-to-day routine, his co-conspirators had assumed the pen was abandoned. How silly! Yet it was not his place to tell them, for they thought him a simpleton. Then the goatherd had arrived the day after the kidnapping. At the time he had thought he had outsmarted him by letting Agnes out to play. Now he realized that perhaps it was he who had been outsmarted.

Plato could see a group hovering around Agnes. Shortly, three figures headed in his direction. Should he run? No, he decided. It was *Bondye's* will that he be captured. It would be his penance. He began chanting rhythmically to *Baron Samedi*. *"Sovi lavi li, sovi lavi li...* (Save her life, save her life...)"

Omart followed close behind a contingent of the Haitian police squad, who approached the door of Plato's home cautiously, with their rifles at the ready. Two stationed themselves on either side of the door, while one hollered, "Open the door and come out with your hands up" in Kreyol.

The police counted to ten and hearing no response, kicked in the door, ready to shoot if they met any resistance. Instead, they found Plato prostrate, face up, eyes wide open but seemingly unresponsive.

"Is he having a seizure?" Omart asked Mathieu, the translator.

"No, I think it's a Vodou thing," Mathieu answered. "Something called a '*seizman.*' The *Lwa* are punishing him..."

Chapter 21
An Escape

“We’ve got her!” Omart exclaimed ebulliently over his cell phone to Jacques and Rose. “She’s sick, exhausted, dehydrated, and hungry, but she’ll be in pretty good shape once we get her to the medical back-up we’ve called to the base of this mountain. She even identified one of the perpetrators – it’s your cook’s husband! I knew it had to be an inside job!”

With this news, Agnes’ parents looked over their shoulders, through the doorway into the kitchen. Josette, either not hearing or not understanding, and with her back towards them, continued her preparation of their noon-time meal. They’d deal with this breach of loyalty later, Jacques decided.

“We’ve captured two others. One’s a local kid – kind of pathetic. They drafted him to serve as a babysitter. We found your wallet and sneakers in his home. We’re not sure who the other guy we’ve caught is – some punk from one of the slum gangs, it seems. There’s another accomplice still at large; your daughter remembers hearing three voices when she was kidnapped and our goatherd got a good visual on the third suspect, probably the ringleader, who spoke in English. You owe this goatherd quite a debt of gratitude, by the way, he really stuck his neck out for your daughter. This is the damndest case I’ve ever worked…”

Upon hearing this, Jacques stiffened a bit. "Oh, I'll see that he's rewarded," he mumbled, annoyed that Omart had even mentioned this. "Where and when can we get her?"

"Come to the embassy in about four hours. We've still got to get down off this mountain, give her some fluids, debrief her, and fill out a report. Here, you can talk to her now, though, if you want."

Since her release, Agnes had alternated between sobbing, shuddering, and hurling Kreyol epithets at Wilson for his betrayal. Michel cradled her in his lap while she shuddered and then restrained her when she attempted to physically assault the family cook's husband.

"*Tranki,*" he murmured. "*Tranki, Li finl* (Rest quietly. It's over!)," he whispered, as he stroked the back of her head and neck.

Wilson huddled in a heap on a rock next to the goat pen, his handcuffed arms covering his head, to protect himself from Agnes' assault. At times, he glared at Michel as if he, not Wilson, were the betrayer. Mostly, he sulked, his dreams of riches and revenge dashed by a goatherd. He was terrified of the prospect of going to jail. Upon reflection, however, he realized that imprisonment in a Haitian jail might be better than the violent death he would suffer at the hands of Ogou for having the stupidity of getting caught, or, for that matter, of suggesting they hide Agnes in a goat pen in the first place. And then there was Josette. On the night of the abduction, it would be discovered later, he had browbeaten her and threatened her with physical violence until she reluctantly agreed to let them in. Now she, too, would go to jail, and their entire family would disown them.

Meanwhile, Plato sobbed tears into his shirt, which he

used to cover his face, while Auguste glowered and postured at his two conspirators, saying with his body language that, if he ever had the chance, he would surely kill them.

At the sound of her father's voice, Agnes composed herself.

"*Papi*?"

"*Ah, ma petite! Merci a Dieu!*"

On hearing Jacques' voice, Wilson sprang from his rock and lunged towards the cell phone, despite the shackles on his feet. It was his one chance to salvage something from this debacle. "*Josette! Ale! Vit! Ale! Vit!*" he screamed at the top of his lungs.

"*Merde!*" exclaimed Jacques as he turned towards the kitchen. Josette was already out the door by the time he could rise from his chair. He tried to follow her as she fled down the hillside street that led from his home to the main square of Petionville, but she was faster. Soon, he lost her in the throngs of market women and customers in *Ti Falluja*.

Omart, still in his body armor, flung himself on top of Wilson, then straddled him and kept him on the ground while one of the Haitian police released the handcuffs and recuffed him with his hands now behind is back. Several minutes passed until Jacques came back on the phone. "Josette got away. I couldn't keep up with her. I'm sorry..."

Josette's escape complicated matters considerably. Omart had hoped that Wilson and Auguste would, under brief but intense interrogation, reveal the identity and location of their ringleader. There was only a small window of opportunity to capture him, for if his accomplices failed to return promptly with the letter signed by Agnes, he would certainly flee. Now that window was closing rapidly. If Josette knew him, she would most likely go there, or if she had access to a phone, she would call him. "Listen, we better start interrogating these guys when we get to the Humvee." He said to his squad, "We better get going!"

As the two squads gathered their gear to begin their descent, Omart glanced back at Agnes and Michel, still hugging one another. *Remarkable,* he thought. *There really are heroes and heroines in this world. People that deserve protecting.* He admired Agnes for the ingenuity she demonstrated in writing her father's number on the back of a shard, using that scrap of charcoal, and the courage of her decision, for the sake of her family's safety, not to flee when Michel first found her.

Michel was even more remarkable, putting his life and the life of his family on the line to save the life of a stranger. An overwhelming sense of responsibility welled up in Omart. If the fourth kidnapper weren't caught, Michel and his family would never be safe in Haiti. He pulled Mathieu aside. "Before we head down, ask our hero if he'd like to come to America."

Chapter 22
The Descent

The hike down the mountain of the F.B.I. team, the Haitian police, their captives, Michel, and Agnes would have been a comical *danse macabre*, were not time of an essence. In fact, Omart's patience with Michel was tested once again as Michel took the time to herd his goats back into the pen and gather their remaining food, placing that inside also. "I don't know when I'll be back again," Michael explained.

Michel carried Agnes down the mountain on his back. Because he was so fit, thanks to his daily routine, even with this burden, he bounded down the path, moving so quickly he had to wait every two hundred yards or so for the others to catch up. Wilson and Auguste, on the other hand, were literally and figuratively dragging their shackled feet. They knew that once they were off the mountain, all hope for escape would be lost, so they turned from side to side, scanning the terrain, looking in vain for some way to evade their captors.

Wilson in particular was stalling, trying to buy Josette as much time as he could to reach Ogou's den. He even faked a limp for a while, forcing the Haitian police guarding him to poke him in the ribs with his rifle butt and remind that he had better behave, as it was still undecided whether he'd be going to a Haitian or American jail. Plato, still paralyzed, had to be carried by two of the Haitian Police; one holding him under his armpits, the other between his knees.

All along the trail, this improbable entourage was greeted by stares of bewildered market women ascending the trail – the goatherd leading the way with a light-skinned child on his back, muscular *blan* with body armor and Haitian police in their standard gear and pressed uniforms, pushing *negs* in handcuffs and shackles ahead of them. It was a day on the trail like no other – so extraordinary that children came running from their homes, laughing and pointing and calling others to witness it.

Michel smiled – not his usual broad, ebullient smile, but rather a sheepish, almost embarrassed one. "I'll explain it all when I see you tomorrow," he said to every passerby. He did not know then that he would never climb the mountain again.

A team of paramedics was waiting at the Humvees. Michel handed over Agnes to them. They quickly started an intravenous line, opened it wide to pour in fluids and piggy-back a small bag containing antibiotics; ordered by their medical back-up at the embassy. They revived Plato with smelling salts. By the time the reluctant prisoners, F.B.I. agents, and Haitian police had loaded themselves into the Humvees, Agnes was fully alert, explaining her ordeal to Omart in thorough detail.

Chapter 23
Cite Soleil

Josette exited the west side of the *Ti Falluja* market. Feigning nonchalance, she had tried not to look distracted or anxious as she weaved through the throngs of market women, with their stacks of onions, eggplants, carrots, and tomatoes, carried there daily from Morne Kenskoff, Feurcy, and La Plaine. Most of them knew her, since she shopped there each morning for fresh produce, and when the doctors were in town, live poultry or goats. She didn't want to raise suspicion that anything was out of the ordinary. Perhaps they wouldn't notice her passing through. When the police arrived, these market women were sure to be questioned, for the doctor had seen her enter the market as she fled down from Petionville *Center-ville*.

Trying to fake some semblance of her daily routine, before continuing her flight down Rue Delmas to Cité Soleil, she lingered at the edge of the market by a truck and pretended to be interested in purchasing one of the doomed chickens, hung upside down by their claws, in rows, from the sideboards of the truck's bonnet. In a country with little refrigeration, custom and concern for sanitation dictated that meat and poultry were purchased live and slaughtered just prior to meal preparation. In the case of these chickens, executions would be carried out by wringing the bird's neck – accomplished by holding the bird's head and twirling its body with a flick of the wrist. Through the years, Josette had a lot of practice in neck-wringing, and that was exactly what she wanted to do at that moment – not to a chicken, but to her husband Wilson!

"I should never have given in to his demands!" she seethed as she negotiated the traffic at the intersection at the top of Rue Delmas. "Him, with his dreams of riches and his arrogance towards the family I worked for, for the past twenty years. Now, we've lost everything. I can't even go home – the police will surely be waiting there. I've got to warn Clarisse. Wilson can rot in jail forever, for all I care, but I won't let that happen to my daughter!"

Josette's fears for her daughter were not unfounded. Even though on face value, she was an innocent victim of her father's scheme, but if she were caught up in the net about to ensnare Ogou and thrown in a Haitian jail, she'd never get out. Even worse, if there were a firefight, Josette had no doubt that Ogou would use Clarisse as a human shield. She knew her husband well – he'd "sing" in fifteen minutes of interrogation or less. There was a small opportunity to warn Clarisse, even if it meant risking her own capture. Perhaps, with luck, her "sugar daddy" wouldn't be there, and they could escape together.

She pulled a few *gourdes* out of her bra (always stashed there for emergencies) and climbed into the back of a *tap-tap* descending Rue Delmas. Although in her mind it took an eternity, she had a bit of luck that day – a combination of no breakdowns, no demonstrations, and a driver skilled in weaving in and out of the Rue Delmas traffic resulted in her getting out at the base of Rue Delmas, a short distance from Cité Soleil, in only twenty minutes.

She jumped over potholes filled with milk chocolate-brown water and weaved swiftly through the crowds on Harry Turman Boulevard near the charcoal market. No reason to be nonchalant here; no one knew her, and they would never see her again.

Just before the main entrance to Cité Soleil, she entered a narrow alleyway – no wider than a person, really, between two cinderblock shells of partially constructed homes. The path zigged and zagged deep into Cité Soleil; at times packed dirt, at times mud, and at times makeshift bridges made of planks set to span particularly large puddles. No sunlight penetrated the alleyway, and the air was acrid with charcoal smoke and pungent with smells of sweat and urine. Josette offered a perfunctory "*bonjou*" to the women bathing their children in washbasins, recycling the bathwater, and the few vendors tucked in corners selling parceled-out portions of spaghetti, sugar, or coffee. She, like Auguste, hated this place; so crowded, so windless, humid, and pest-infested – a hell compared to Petionville's heaven, sitting by the port, at sea level, a festering cauldron of moral and biological disease.

Unbeknown to Wilson and Ogou, Clarisse had been calling her mother throughout her captivity, using Ogou's cellphone in the middle of the night when his snoring told her he had passed out from too much rum. Clarisse pleaded with her mother to come and rescue her. In reality, Josette was powerless until now to help her. She did, however, have the foresight to ask her daughter how she might find her just in case an opportunity arose to set her free. At first, Clarisse had no answer, for Cité Soleil is a maze of ramshackle shacks and alleys. She prayed to *Erzilie* to deliver her. One day, peering through the space left between two sheets of tin, she saw the answer to her prayers. She shared it with her mother that night.

"Go to St. Catherine's Hospital and follow the spliced electrical line about hundred meters. That's where you'll find me."

Josette had never been in Cité Soleil before, but everyone knew where St. Catherine's was; it was the only functioning health care facility in the slum, the place most of Cité Soleil's mothers delivered their babies. Every time she reached a seeming dead end, a resident, seeing the pain on her face, would send her off in the right direction, each having been taught as a child to never leave a stranger in distress.

When she reached the hospital, she circled it once. Sure enough, behind the hospital was a line of utility poles and off one a spliced single wire that drooped over an alleyway and then ran along the rooftops. She followed the line until it disappeared into a four-room shack. Josette took a deep breath, then pushed through the door.

"Get dressed!" she barked at her daughter, Clarisse, who happened to be in the first of the collection of shacks that Ogou called his headquarters. "They've caught your father and the police will be here any minute. I'm taking you with me into hiding in *Kafou*. Is the idiot here?"

Ogou emerged from the latrine, zipping the fly of his designer jeans as he reentered his lair. "What?" he exclaimed.

"You stupid, stupid fool!" Josette stammered. "You picked on American citizens who called the F.B.I.! They've rescued the girl and captured Wilson. If I know him, he'll be leading them in here in just a few minutes. You need to get out of here. You also need to give Clarisse and me some money – she's not going with you – we're going to disappear and start again in *Kafou* (Carrefour, the largest suburb of Port-au-Prince)."

Astonished, Ogou wasted only a second, then turned towards his dresser drawer. He pulled out his pistol, stuffed his pockets with ammunition and then took out several cigar boxes, each sealed with duct tape and containing about $10,000. All but one were placed in a gunnysack along with some hastily thrown-in jeans and T-shirts. The one remaining box he gave to Clarisse. To say Ogou was not generous by nature would be an understatement. He did not want Clarisse to get caught – she had overheard too much about his business dealings in general and the kidnapping plans in particular. He thought for an instant about killing them, but he knew the police would soon be bearing down on him. Going to jail for kidnapping was one thing but getting a lethal injection for a double murder was another. No, better to buy them off and leave quickly. Besides, if he were caught, giving Clarisse money changed her from sex-slave to whore – one less charge to worry about.

"Thanks for everything, sugar," he murmured as he handed her the box and kissed her on the cheek. "This should tide you and your mom over for a little while. We'll meet up again when this all quiets down." This show of affection and generosity was more for Josette than Clarisse's sake, but Josette would have none of it.

"Not if I can help it!" exclaimed Josette, snatching the box from Clarisse's hands. "Don't bother packing," she said, turning to Clarisse. "We don't have time. We'll use this to buy new clothes once we're settled in *Kafou.*"

The three of them left together down the alleyway but set off in opposite directions when they got to Boulevard Harry Truman. Josette and Clarisse walked about five kilometers to *Kafou*, (written in French as "Carrefour" on the maps, but pronounced "*Kafou*" in Kreyol), a sprawling community, part city, part slum that straddles along both sides of the coastal road and up a hillside just south of Port-au-Prince. With over a million people living there, *Kafou* is the most densely packed suburb of the most densely packed capitol of the most densely packed country in the Western Hemisphere. They could hide out among the masses there forever, Josette reasoned, renting a room in a cheap hotel until they could find an apartment and new work in the upscale neighborhood of *Paco* just above *Kafou*.

As soon as Ogou was out of sight, he headed for a *tap-tap* station and boarded a bus heading for Gonaives; a port city about three hours north of Port-au-Prince. There were lots of abandoned houses there, thanks to a flood that almost destroyed the town a year before. The rebellion against Aristide had started there, driving away the police. Between the flood and the rebellion, it was a lawless place – a good place to reestablish his drug connections. Yes, it was another hellhole, but no worse than Cité Soleil; a hellhole-cum-safe haven. Besides, he reasoned, with plenty of desperate young girls and his cigar boxes of cash, he would soon be living the high life again.

Chapter 24
Crossroads

Josette's assessment of her husband's ability to withstand interrogation was correct. All it took was Omart, in his "good cop" role, to offer incarceration in an American jail as opposed to a Haitian jail for Wilson to volunteer to lead the F.B.I. team directly to Ogou's lair.

The trip from the base of the mountain to the embassy – the team had to drop off Agnes and Michel before venturing into Cité Soleil – seemed interminable to Omart. He was all too aware that Josette's escape in all probability gave him only a small chance of capturing the ring-leader – a mysterious figure Wilson could only identify by his first name, Ogou.

Despite his impatience, however, Omart couldn't help but be taken in with the panoply of Haitian life that played out as their Humvee inched through *La Plaine* and *Post Cazeau* and finally down Boulevard Harry Truman to the embassy. The embassy was just east of the entrance to Cité Soleil and just north of the suburb of *Kafou* on the road that coursed along the edge of Port-au-Prince's harbor and its largest slums.

Most of his time in Haiti had been spent in the Hotel Montana, with occasional forays to restaurants in Petionville and down Rue Pan Americain to the embassy to review police reports or to the morgue, on the grounds of the University Hospital. Rue Pan Americain, which, along with Rue Delmas, linked Petionville to Haiti's capital, was a conduit for Haiti's elite and middle class to and from their jobs in Port-au-Prince each day. As such, the trip from the Montana to the embassy was, in Omart's opinion, somewhat mundane and boring – the same clogging of the roadways with SUVs, the same foot traffic of uniformed school children and starched-shirt office workers. These roads were different; throngs of people carrying on the lifeblood of the economy of the capital right there on the streets; bringing in food, making furniture, repairing cars, selling clothes, buying charcoal, making cinder blocks. On and on, this seemingly endless panoply of life stretched the entire ten miles between Croix-de-Bouquets and the embassy. The sea of humanity, all trying to survive, impressed upon Omart even more than he originally appreciated the extraordinariness of Michel's commitment to free Agnes. If they didn't capture this Ogou character, Michel's life and the lives of his family would be forever in danger. Omart would have no recourse but to bring them all to Miami and enroll them in the Witness Protection Program. He urged his driver on, even if it meant chasing a few pedestrians and cyclists off the road. There was not much he could do, however, when they got to Boulevard Harry Truman. A large *tap-tap* with a sign saying "Port-au-Prince – Gonaives" was loading passengers and baggage, blocking one lane of the boulevard. Precious minutes were lost.

Agnes, exhausted by starvation, dehydration, and five nights of fitful sleep in the goat pen had fallen asleep in Michel's arms in the back of the Humvee. Were she not sleeping, she might have seen Josette and Clarisse (she grew up with Clarisse) weaving through the boulevard's pedestrian traffic, heading to *Kafou*, just before they arrived at the embassy.

Omart flashed his credentials to the embassy guard and asked them to escort Agnes and Michel to the ambassador's conference room. Rousing Agnes, he told her that her parents would be waiting there for her. To Michel, he explained through Matthieu that he'd return for him as soon as possible. Their Humvee then set out on the short excursion into Cité Soleil, followed by two SUVs full of Haitian National Police.

The people of Cité Soleil that they passed along the way (and there were thousands) wore facial expressions ranging from sullen to outright hostile, with the intrusion of yet another police caravan into the heart of the shantytown. Since President Aristide's departure, hardly a day passed without some appearance by either the police or the UN peacekeeping forces looking for *chimeres* or drug dealers. Even on days in which there were no incursions, the UN convoys were permanently posted at the entryways of the slum, attempting to isolate and contain its citizens almost as if they were under quarantine. The interim government believed that if there were to be a counter-rebellion, it would come from Cité Soleil, and the slums like it nearby, so they sought to isolate the people there and contain unrest almost as if that unrest were a plague. Of course, that attempt proved futile, since the blockades could only control the flow of vehicular traffic, and hardly anyone in Cité Soleil owned a vehicle. The people of Cité Soleil entered and left on foot, at will, through the hundreds of alleys and foot paths that separated the rows of shacks.

The convoy parked in front of Ste. Catherine's hospital and, arms at the ready, set out on foot. Wilson led, followed by the Haitian police, with the F.B.I. team bringing up the rear. In five minutes, Wilson, still in shackles, had led them to the cluster of shacks that served as Ogou's den. After pointing to it silently, he retreated behind the rear phalanx of officers. The police surrounded the complex. Then, the lead officer called out for anyone inside to come out with their hands up. No response came forth, and after several minutes and a second calling, the police, rather than barging through the open doorway, smashed through a cardboard side wall. They searched in every room, including the latrine, and even shined a flashlight down the latrine hole. There was no one there, although the pile of clothes, a half empty bottle of rum and the smell of fresh urine wafting out of the latrine hole suggested that Ogou had hastily and just recently departed.

"Damn!" shouted Omart as he punched his fist through another side wall. Returning to the convoy, however, his equanimity returned. They had rescued the child unharmed. That was the most important thing. After such a close call, it would be a while, if ever, before Ogou tried kidnapping again, he reasoned, and Wilson, Plato, and Auguste would be going to prison for a long time. Michel would be able to give up goat-herding and start a new life for himself and his family in Miami.

I'll want to be there to settle him in and show him around, Omart thought. *I'll bet he'll think he died and went to Heaven...*

Chapter 25
Miami

The next day, Omart escorted Michel one last time to Lamardelle, to say goodbye to his mother and his other family members. After he explained in detail what happened, his mother rose and kissed him.

"I'm very proud of you," she said.

"I did what I was taught to do – I couldn't just leave her there!" Michel responded.

He gave his house and his goats to his younger brother, who had just turned sixteen. "If you care for them (the goats) well, they'll give you a decent living," he told him. "You'll be able to court a girl and start a family in no time. With any luck, you'll find someone as wonderful as Cheri." He then took his mother aside and whispered in her ear, "I don't know if we'll ever be back, but I'll send money as soon as I'm working. Maybe, someday, I'll be able to bring you to Miami also. In the meantime, here's the *ti cob* we'd been saving to send Jean-Peter to school. We won't need it now. School in Miami is free!"

It took two weeks to create a new identity for Michel, including a passport, a social security number, and a Florida driver's license. This last item was particularly specious since Michel had never driven a vehicle in his life. He needed a photo ID other than his passport for the Witness Protection Program; however, and a driver's license made the most sense.

Omart and his crew helped pass the time between Agnes' liberation and their departure to Miami by giving Michel driving lessons; first in the Hotel Montana parking lot and then progressively longer and more adventurous excursions, up and down Rue Pan-Americain, across Petionville, and up the mountain to Kenskoff village and Fuercy.

After much discussion, Omart and Michel decided his new name would be Patrice Rousseau. Like most Haitians, Michel had always admired pictures of St. Patrick driving the snakes out of Ireland – not that he knew where Ireland was or that St. Patrick himself had spent his youth as a slave, like Michel's ancestors. Rather, in his mind, the snakes represented Danballah, the Vodou snake god. "Rousseau," borrowed from the French philosopher, was Omart's idea.

Michel's wife, Cheri, would not be able to get her new identity in time to accompany Michel to Miami. He was needed as quickly as possible in Miami for an arraignment of Nelson, Plato, and Auguste. The couple understood that they would be apart for some time, and in the time before his departure for Miami, Cheri showed her pride for his heroism by showering him with affection. The two weeks spent at the Montana were almost like a honeymoon for the "love birds," as Omart and his crew called them. In fact, Cheri conceived their second child during their stay there.

Omart volunteered to be Michel's protector/bodyguard for the Witness Protection Program in Miami. In anticipation of this role, he needed to be physically with or near Michel the entire time he stayed at Montana, traveled to Miami, and settled in there. He enjoyed being Michel's protector and mentor as to all things modern. It meant he could give up the drudgery of daily visits to the morgue and review of Haitian police reports. Michel's testimony would be critical to the prosecution of the three kidnappers already in custody. Omart felt some responsibility, however, that the ringleader was still at large, and that responsibility made him even more committed to Michel's safety. Furthermore, having witnessed the whole improbable story, he felt "the system" owed Michel protection for the risks he took in rescuing Agnes. He would personally guarantee that security. Secretly, however, the real reason for his enjoyment was he so liked being around Michel. He was so sincere, naïve, and affable. Plus, Omart liked "showing him the ropes" – teaching him the things he needed to know for his new life and watching Michel's wonder of these new things unfold.

As the day of their departure approached, Omart took Michel shopping for clothes and began daily classes in rudimentary English. These preparations for life in Miami went smoothly. Attempts to teach him about U.S. currency, banking, and American culture were more problematic.

On the morning of departure, Omart suited up Michel in jeans, sneakers, a Marlins baseball cap, and t-shirt. Things went reasonably well in the Port-au-Prince airport – Omart simply prompting Michel to follow him through the process of getting his boarding pass, passing through customs, the x-ray machines, and finally actually boarding the plane. Omart arranged for Michel to have a window seat and explained to the flight attendant that it was his first airplane flight ever. The force of acceleration and the noise of the engines as the plane took off momentarily surprised Michel and he gripped the armrests intensely. Shortly after take-off, however, Michel relaxed and became absorbed with the beauty unfolding out the window below him – the mountains of Haiti's north, the islands of Turks and Caicos, and the myriad hues of the waters of the Bahama Banks.

Michel cheered and clapped with the other passengers when their plane arrived in Miami. From there, things went downhill. He was perplexed by the urinal flushing via an electric light sensor, stymied as to where to place his foot as he attempted to mount the escalator, and dumbfounded as customs agents barked commands in English only. In each instance, Omart, with help from his translator, Mathieu, patiently tried to explain these experiences and ease the transition.

Prior to coming to Miami, Michel had thought he had experienced the gamut of pedestrian and vehicular traffic in Croix-de-Bouquets, whose narrow streets were almost always locked in perpetual semi-gridlock. However, the sheer number of cars on Interstate 95, the speed at which they traveled, and the surprising phenomenon of only one or two people per car, coupled with the opulence of most cars and the reflection of the evening sun off the skyline of the city of Miami in front of them overwhelmed him.

In order to keep Michel's location a secret from any possible accomplices Ogou might have in Little Haiti, F.B.I. Headquarters decided to put Michel up in an apartment in Liberty City – a predominately African-American community just to the west. This proved to be a mistake, for Michel could not communicate well with his neighbors. Some of these neighbors, perhaps earning a living through not entirely legal means, viewed with suspicion the daily visits of Omart and his team. Soon, there were threats scrawled on his apartment door. Angry men would scream at him when he passed them on the street. Michel wasn't quite sure what they were saying, but he could tell from their raised voices, facial expressions, and gestures that they were not pleased with this presence.

Omart appealed Headquarters' decision. Headquarters

assumed that with his black skin, Michel would blend right into Liberty City. Omart knew better. At best, his inability to speak English and Haitian mannerisms would single him out. Perhaps someone might offer him drugs, and who knows, in his naiveté, Michel might accept them.

Omart convinced his SAC (Special Agent in Charge) that Michel would be better off in Little Haiti. Eventually, he'd have to assimilate, and that assimilation would be easier there. Besides, he argued, what intelligence they had gathered through interrogation of Wilson and Auguste indicated that Ogou's U.S. roots were in New York, not Miami.

Meanwhile, Michel was becoming deeply depressed. He couldn't go out, he couldn't talk to his neighbors. The conveniences Omart taught him to use in his apartment – the TV remote, VCR, and cell phone – meant nothing to him. He missed his family, he missed his daily climb up Morne Kenskoff, with its spectacular vistas. Miami was so flat! He even missed his goats! To ease his transition, the Witness Protection Program provided him and his family in Haiti with cellphones. His bill for his first month came to $600.00! The daily visits by Omart, their outings to the beach, to the ballpark, to headquarters, to Burger King, and to his English classes cheered him only slightly. That irrepressible smile that so impressed Omart in Haiti at times evaporated.

Though Miami was not what Michel expected, he never wavered in his resolve to see through his commitment to Omart and Agnes, to see that justice was served. He had to tell his story often – to other F.B.I. agents, to prosecutors, and to defense attorneys. For these interviews, he shook off his lethargy and recounted his story with enthusiasm and attention to detail. He would be a great witness, Omart thought, as he watched a public defender's futile attempts to crack his story during a deposition. If only Miami doesn't break him first in the six months until trial.

Miami F.B.I. headquarters is located just off interstate 95, about three miles north of Little Haiti. Its exterior is non-descript; it could easily be mistaken for a bank or office complex, but once inside, it's very much like being in a bunker. Omart now realized that he himself had been afflicted by a bunker mentality. Neither he nor his fellow agents had any knowledge of Little Haiti or where to find Michel an apartment there. Fortunately, many of the support staff – the janitors, cleaning ladies, and security guards – were Haitian-American. When Omart told them Michel's story, they all volunteered to help.

Through word of mouth of these volunteers, Omart found an apartment in Little Haiti in an ideal location – a duplex on a Haitian church property opposite a school. Michel's mood improved quickly after he moved in. He soon engaged in daily conversations with his neighbors and nightly discussions with the pastor on matters of theology. Things improved even more two weeks later, when Cheri and Jean-Peter finally arrived. Michel was elated to learn that Cheri was carrying his second child. Relieved that he had rescued his star witness from the culture shock of Miami, the dangers of Liberty City, and the depths of depression, Omart settled into a routine of shepherding his adopted family through their daily routines of English classes, job training, doctor visits, shopping, and trips to the movies. In the process, they became the most improbable of friends.

Chapter 26
Justice

In the end, between Wilson and Plato's confessions and Michel's deposition, as well as the physical evidence, no trial was necessary. Omart, who led the interrogations, had thought he had heard it all in his twenty-five years as an F.B.I. Special Agent. This story, however, left him flabbergasted. Wilson was a distant cousin of Jacques, a kinship which Wilson believed gave him a certain entitlement. "After all, family is everything," he would remind Jacques whenever he fell on hard times, which happened all too frequently. If the truth be known, he had always been a little jealous of Jacques' and Rose's success – not just that they went to medical school, but also had the good fortune to emigrate to the United States. Wilson's only secure source of money was Josette's salary, and she was, as their daughter got older, increasingly reluctant to share that with him. Instead, she had put that money aside for Clarisse's schooling. He had been working for President Aristide, nominally as a "poll worker," but that work evaporated when the president left the country. His request to Jacques for employment – perhaps as a chauffeur or general handyman – was scoffed at. "I already have a reliable chauffeur, and I pay your wife full-time to cook and clean for us, in spite of the fact that we're rarely here!" was Jacques' response. It wasn't so much Jacques' words that set Wilson off.

It was the lack of respect. There was no excuse for that, Wilson thought. After all, he was family. In his mind, not showing respect was a sin worse than the crime of kidnapping! After this perceived slight, he ruminated daily as to how he might get revenge, co-mingled with the thought as to how he might get some money from Jacques and Rose. That's how the plot to kidnap Agnes was born.

He claimed he wished no harm for Agnes. She played with his daughter growing up, he exclaimed, and he was just seeking vengeance for Jacques' social slight and some money to tide him over the hard times. It was only as the plan unfolded under Ogou that things spun out of control.

To succeed, Ogou told him, they'd need to have a team and a well-thought-out plan. Ogou would be responsible for the plan and would supply the drug to sedate their victim. Auguste would oversee "the extraction" and ransom negotiations. Wilson would need to create a breach in security, so they could enter the family compound. They'd need someone to watch over the child and a secure location to hide her. It was then that Wilson volunteered the goat-pens near Granthier, a small village where he grew up on the back side of Kenskoff Mountain. "No one would ever think to look for her there," he had told Ogou and Auguste.

Ogou asked how much they might be able to demand in ransom. "Well, both the mother and father are practicing doctors in Brooklyn and they have a big home there and a home in Petionville. I'd say at least $200,000."

At this point in the interrogation, Wilson broke down. "I'll need a down payment," Ogou demanded. "After all, professionals don't work for free, and there's always the chance that something will go wrong and we'll get no cash out on the backend."

"When I told him I had no money, he asked if I had any children!" Wilson sobbed. "I thought he was joking! So, the whole deal depended on me delivering my daughter, Clarisse, to them. It was almost as if they were holding her for ransom, so that I wouldn't back out or lose my nerve. I told my wife, Josette, that I found Clarisse some work as a live-in servant. Once Clarisse was there, though, I don't want to think about what they did to her. My wife saw right through it after the first day; I think Clarisse might have called her, using his cell phone while he was asleep. By then, it was too late. That's how they got Josette to go along with the plan. They told us they'd kill our daughter. That's the only thing that would force my wife to be quiet. She's a good woman and very loyal to Jacques and Rose. If you find Josette and Clarisse, tell them I'm sorry. They're innocent! If you find them, please don't throw them in a Haitian jail!"

Omart, as skilled as he was in interrogation and as well-trained in controlling his emotions, struggled to restrain himself as Wilson's confession unfolded. After all, he had children also. How could this ill-formed desire for revenge, salted with a dream of riches, blind him to the presence of evil incarnate in this villain Ogou? Granted, Wilson was poor, but Michel was even poorer. Thanks to Josette's salary, he was hardly desperate. The contrast between the two and the choices they made almost became an obsession to Omart, but he resolved to put it out of his mind.

These questions are best left to philosophers, not special agents, he thought as he refocused on the interrogation.

Plato's confession was another matter. Omart felt a modicum of pity for him. He was eighteen at the time of his arrest. He never attended school and could neither read nor write. When his parents could no longer feed his brothers and sisters in Granthier, they moved down to Croix de Bouquets, leaving Plato to watch over their ancestral home. He believed Auguste initially, when he was told he'd be given a job as a baby-sitter. He never questioned, until it was too late, why a child from Petionville would need to be hidden in a goat pen in Granthier, of all places. Once recruited, he also was told he'd be killed if he didn't do as he was told. That was no excuse, he admitted – what he did was wrong, it went against everything his family had taught him. That's why he let Agnes out of the pen, in spite of the fact that if Ogou found out about her release, he might be murdered. One must never leave a stranger in distress, he'd been taught.

Auguste sat stone-faced and silent during his interrogation. His court-appointed attorney had advised him to remain silent. In truth, there was little he could do that would help his defense. His lawyer did her best to discredit Wilson – a liar who delivered his own daughter into sex-slavery, who plea-bargained and incriminated Auguste to save his own neck, she claimed, and Plato – a gullible, uneducated youth whose testimony could not be trusted. She could not, however, discredit the testimony of Michel.

Omart, attending the deposition as a silent observer, was so proud of Michel – he proved to be a star witness, identifying Auguste and Wilson as two of the three men he overheard discussing murdering someone as they descended the trail from his goat pen, recounting their conversation verbatim, as well as his conversation with Agnes. He then withstood a blistering assault by Auguste's attorney, who tried unsuccessfully to raise doubts about the veracity of his recollections and to suggest that the whole story was just too improbable to be true.

"Why didn't you just take the girl with you?"

"She didn't want to leave because she feared for her family."

"Whose idea was it to make cement blocks to pay for the phone call?"

"It was mine. I didn't have the heart to tell the girl I had no phone and no money. I didn't want to take away her hope."

"Did you expect a reward? Did the F.B.I. tell you if you identified my client you'd get to come to the United States?"

"No. I did what I did because it was the right thing to do," he answered matter-of-factly. "My grandparents taught me never to leave a stranger in distress. I didn't want to come here to Miami, but one of the kidnappers escaped, so my family was in danger. I had to come for them."

The final nails in Auguste's coffin were the physical evidence. As it turned out, probably by design, Ogou had provided Wilson and Auguste with toy guns, not real ones. These were discovered in the Trailblazer left at the crest of the mountain when they were apprehended. They were covered with Wilson's and Auguste's fingerprints. Also found in the Trailblazer was Agnes' bed sheet, with fibers matching those removed from Auguste's shirt and jeans and Wilson's machete, which he had pressed against Agnes' neck on the night of the abduction. Finally, there was the letter Auguste forced Agnes to sign the day they were captured. Omart kept a straight face as he presented this evidence to the public defenders. When it was over, however, he allowed himself the slightest of smiles. This time, justice would be served.

Epilogue

Kidnappings remained common during the interim government that ruled Haiti after the departure of President Aristide. As a result of the "Agnes affair" however, word spread rapidly on the street – make sure your intended victim is not a U.S. citizen. If they were, you risked being tracked down by the *Biwo Investigasion Fedwal*!

In the months following the election of President Preval in 2006, order was restored, and the number of kidnappings diminished. UN troops continued to be stationed on the outskirts of Cité Soleil and the other slums of Port-au-Prince. In reality, their presence accomplished little. Surprisingly, kidnappings did not recur after the earthquake that devastated Haiti in January of 2010. There was, however, a brief increase in cases in the months leading up to the election of President Martelly in 2011. Most likely, these were, in large part, politically motivated. Kidnapping surged, however, following President Moise' assassination. In September 2021 alone, there were more than six hundred.

The whereabouts of Josette, Clarisse, and Ogou were never discovered. It's quite possible that Josette and Clarisse died in the earthquake that ravaged Port-au-Prince in January of 2010 – *Kafou* was the community most severely affected by the quake, with the highest loss of life. It's also possible Ogou died in the cholera epidemic that ravaged the cities of St. Marc and Gonaives in 2010 and 2011. A small bit of good news; little earthquake damage or cholera occurred in Lamardelle, where Michel and Cheri's family still reside. Michel, true to his word, sent monthly remittances to his mother once he started working. In spite of attempted interventions by the F.B.I. and Witness Protection Program, however, she was repeatedly denied a visa, failing to prove she had a compelling interest to return to Haiti after the visa expired. She and Michel have not seen each other since he left.

Auguste was sentenced to twenty-five years for kidnapping. Wilson received a lesser sentence of fifteen years, as an accessory to the crime – a plea deal arranged by Omart as a result of his cooperation with the investigation and his willingness to testify against Auguste and Plato. Plato also received a reduced sentence – the judge believed he expressed genuine remorse and was also impressed with the fact that he let Agnes out of the pen to play with other children.

After his sentencing, Plato withdrew emotionally, speaking to no one, doing nothing, barely eating. He attempted suicide by hanging himself with his bed sheet in his cell. A court psychiatrist declared him deeply depressed, but competent to stand trial. Medication did nothing to relieve his depression. A Kreyol-speaking chaplain, however, took pity on him and visited him frequently, ultimately hearing his confession and assigning as penance that he learn to read and write.

Jacques, Rose, and Agnes returned to Brooklyn shortly after Agnes' liberation. Jacques, vowing they would never return to Haiti, put their home in Petionville on the market, eventually selling it at a loss. He refused to let Agnes talk to Omart or to prosecutors, declaring that she had been through enough. He did, however, allow her to write Michel a thank you note, care of Omart at Miami F.B.I., in which he enclosed a check for five hundred dollars.

"That's a pretty small reward for the man that saved our daughter's life!" exclaimed Rose, taken aback by her husband's apparent stinginess and lack of gratitude.

"That's at least twice what he earned in a year as a goatherd," Jacques countered. "The F.B.I. is supporting him now in Miami. That's more of a reward than we could ever give him! Besides, he's Haitian. He didn't rescue her for a reward, he did it because his grandparents and parents taught him never to leave a stranger in distress!"

Michel rapidly learned English and passed his driving test to earn an authentic license on his first try. Omart saw to it that the Witness Protection Program bought him a car and arranged for him to get a job as a custodian in a school. Seven months after her arrival in Miami, his wife gave birth to their second child, a son. They named him Omart. Life in Miami, however, was not the cornucopia of delights that Omart anticipated it would be for Michel and Cheri. It was particularly difficult for Cheri; confined to home and walking distance from home – she could never master driving and the streets of Miami terrified her – and forced to raise her children without the support of her extended family. Michel tried to help as much as he could, taking the car for groceries after work and carrying his family to church services at Notre Dame D'Haiti church on Sundays. Over time, however, her unhappiness strained their relationship. She has requested to return to Haiti – over Michel's objections – but the Witness Protection Program denied that request.

In the spring of 2011, the U.S. Immigration and Customs

Enforcement Agency resumed deportation of convicted felons to Haiti. The deportations had been suspended by the State Department for humanitarian reasons after the January 2010 earthquake. Initially, these felons were deported directly to Haitian prisons. Human rights groups complained vociferously via appeals to the United Nations at the Organization of American States – some "felons" were guilty of no more than traffic violations and some of the initial deportees died shortly after arrival from cholera and other infectious diseases. As a result of these appeals, policy was changed and deportees were released directly to "the community" – a community with over 500,000 people still homeless and living in the streets. Plato, Auguste, and Wilson were among these "direct releases." Plato found his way to a seminary and studied for the priesthood. Authorities have lost track of Wilson and Auguste. At the time of this writing, their whereabouts are unknown.

2010: Unsung Heroes

Preface

Dr. Barth Green, Chair of Neurosurgery at the University of Miami Miller School of Medicine and the person who founded Medishare with me in 1994, likes to boast that he was the first University of Miami faculty on the ground after the 2010 earthquake, arriving by private plane one day later. Without detracting from Dr. Green's heroic response to the quake, he is wrong. Dr. André Vulcain, in the Department of Family Medicine, and Marie Chery, of the School of Nursing, were both in-country during the quake and played heroic roles in the quake's immediate aftermath. In addition, Marie was at the vanguard of the response to the cholera epidemic that erupted ten months later. In fact, the University of Miami's successes after the quake would not have been possible without the Haitian and Haitian-American faculty that worked with Medishare for years prior to the quake. Their stories are laced with questions of theodicy and the power of individuals to fight evil, despite overwhelming odds.

Chapter 27
Eyewitness

At first, with his eyes closed, Dr. André Vulcain thought he must be having an acute attack of vertigo, so violent was the sensation that his head was spinning. Yes, vertigo, perhaps brought on by fatigue and dehydration. He had awoken in the middle of the night to catch the first flight from Miami to Port-au-Prince, then rushed to the Aeroport General, hoping to catch an early flight to Cap Haitian to attend an important meeting at the hospital there the following morning. First, however, he had to rendezvous with his brother. His brother was traveling to New York that day and it being the middle of January, André wanted him to have his winter coat.

Of course, the two brothers spent some time catching up on family matters. Their conversation outside the airport took longer than he expected. By the time he arrived at the general airport, it was already afternoon. André, meticulously careful, had made a study of the flights to Cap Haitian and their track record of safety. As the sun heated up the mountains in the approach to Cap Haitian, the trade winds, forced upward, caused turbulence and afternoon thunderstorms. These storms tossed the small 20-seat turboprops flying to Cap Haitian around like butterflies. Traveling to and from Haiti so often, André always took care to avoid disaster. Crashes of the Cap Haitian commuter planes only happened in the afternoon, so he never flew in the afternoon. He was conflicted, however, by the fact that he had that important meeting to attend.

"What's the weather in Cap Haitian?" he asked the clerk at the Caribintair counter.

"It's raining, Dr. Vulcain," she answered. She, like all the clerks, knew him well – he made the trip so often, up and back every month for the last ten years, supervising, managing, and always worrying about the Family Medicine Residency Training Program that the University of Miami Miller School of Medicine founded there in 1998.

André attended medical school in Haiti and trained there as a surgeon. After residency, he worked as a surgeon and Medical Director at the hospital in the small city of Fort Liberte, a few kilometers east of Cap Haitian. There, he became aware that his surgical training had not prepared him for what his patients really needed; preventative medicine, health education, and simple remedies for common but potentially lethal illnesses.

He was a patriot in the best sense of the word – acutely aware of Haiti's unique history and dedicated to improving its present sad state of health care. During his lunch break each day, he would leave the clinic and go to the old fort, built by the French, to meditate. It was during one of these meditations that he realized what Haiti needed were not specialists, but rather, well-trained generalists who could take care of most of the problems the people faced. He vowed to study further, prepare for the licensure exam (the Flex), come to the United States, and train to be a family doctor. After training, he would return to Haiti to introduce the discipline there.

It's a little-known fact that modern Family Medicine began, in large part, in Miami – the first Department of Family Medicine was founded there in 1966 and the first Family Medicine Residency Training Program started there in 1967.

André completed his training in 1997. When the School of Medicine received a grant from the Open Society Institute to start a family medicine training program in Haiti in 1998, André was the logical person to lead that effort. For André, it was a dream come true. To make that dream a reality, however, would take twelve years of devotion and a Herculean effort, including spending two weeks out of every month in Haiti.

When the spinning didn't stop, André opened his eyes and stared at the ceiling of his hotel room, hoping to suppress the nauseating sensation of vertigo. He soon, however, realized the truth; it was not vertigo but an earthquake that caused the spinning! Fearing the building might collapse on him, he grabbed his trousers and stumbled out the door.

The Visa Lodge Hotel, where he decided to stay after he rescheduled his flight, is a collection of one-story bungalows surrounding a two-story bar, restaurant, and pool deck. It is located near the airport, north of Port-au-Prince. The epicenter of the quake was south of the city, so the hotel itself did not suffer major damage. Even so, the shaking was violent enough that all the patrons exited their bungalows in various stages of undress. One patron at the bar thought he was having an alcoholic hallucination – the quake caused a mini-tsunami, with the pool emptying itself and drenching him with a wall of water, hurled at him from fifty feet away. The quake was followed by complete silence – a phenomenon unheard of in the usually traffic-congested location of the hotel near the airport. Then after a minute, the patrons all heard a massive collective groan. A cloud of dust rose from the ground to the sky, obliterating the sun and creating a haze of red and blue – ironically, the colors of the Haitian flag, symbol of a nation whose capital had just vaporized into dust.

Chapter 28
Moonscape

Perhaps it was the lights powered by the Visa Lodge's emergency generators or perhaps it was its silhouette that suggested a large intact structure that might provide shelter, but shortly after dark a swelling stream of injured people ascended the slight rise above the Airport Road to the hotel grounds. Injuries ranged from minor lacerations to compound fractures. Some people staggered in on their own, while others were carried in by neighbors or strangers – shell shocked but with enough presence of mind to organize themselves as voluntary First Responders. All were covered by a chalky white cement dust, giving them a ghost-like appearance.

André always carried some medical supplies in his bag – items he scrounged from the Family Practice Center in Miami; sutures, scalpels, gauze pads, latex gloves, and the like. They were needed supplies for his residency program in Cap Haitian. He set about, therefore, triaging patients and administering first aid; washing wounds with soap and water, dressing them with gauze, setting simple fractures and suturing lacerations. Those severely injured, he instructed to head to the emergency room of the University Hospital in downtown Port-au-Prince, not knowing it was severely damaged by the quake and had no medical or nursing staff on duty. The night passed in what seemed both an instant and eternity – hundreds of patients scattered around the pool-patio, in what became an open-air urgent care center.

By the time the sun rose, when he had treated all the patients he could at the Visa Lodge, he decided to go with friends to check on his sister-in-law, niece and their home in the upscale neighborhood of Bourbon, on the other side of the capital. From there, he could try to phone home and let his wife, Babette, know he was all right. He had a truck and a tank of gas, but he had to make it last – who knew how long it would take for essential services to be restored?

The neighborhoods near the airport and the Visa Lodge showed some damage, but still had recognizable structures, giving André hope that perhaps the damage was not as severe as he first feared. As he got closer to the center of the city, however, debris littered the streets and the dead lined the sidewalks, neatly arranged with arms folded by passers-by who knew the importance to Haitians of respect for the dead. Some people were feverishly digging through the rubble looking for loved ones or trying to free victims trapped below. Others wandered about aimlessly. Even those fortunate few who owned homes that somehow survived stayed outside, usually huddling around outdoor cooking fires. The closer he got to downtown, the thicker the dust became and the greater the number of bodies neatly arranged by survivors. Rue Delmas, usually bustling with traffic, was deserted and impossible to navigate; seemingly every edifice flattened like a crepe. It was a moonscape.

André decided it would be impossible to take his usual route home. Instead, he and his friends took a series of back roads, which ascended a valley between two hills to his neighborhood.

Ironically, Boulevard Harry Truman had less debris than other roads in Port-au-Prince. Bordered on its West by Cite Soleil, the poorest and most crowded slum in the Western Hemisphere, turned out to be something of a blessing – cardboard and tin provided much more resilience to a 7.0 magnitude earthquake than un-reinforced concrete. There were even a few market women along the boulevard, manning their stalls and hoping to sell some wares.

Haitians are a people that live on hope. Whatever hope the relative sparing of the neighborhoods near the Visa Lodge may have raised in André's heart was drowned as he rounded a turn and passed in front of the presidential palace. Built by United States Marines during their occupation of Haiti in 1930, it always conveyed to André an aura of indestructibility. Now, one wing had collapsed, leaving the dome dangling like a bowler hat on a hat rack. Across the street, Champs Mars, the large public plaza, was swarmed with tens of thousands of newly homeless people. Some stood in shock, while others gathered in groups, arms extended, singing hymns and whispering prayers.

It was now around eleven. The tropical sun filtering through the dust created an eerie yellow haze. The entrance to the emergency room of the University Hospital had collapsed, as well as a wing of the hospital that contained the surgical suites, rendering the hospital, in effect, useless. A crowd clamored outside, calling futilely for help, for the medical and nursing staff had either been killed, injured, or left to seek out and try to save their own families.

Around the corner from the University Hospital were the public medical school and nursing school, now completely caved in. Decades of tensions between the government and the medical profession over support for the hospital and medical school led to frequent strikes. Indeed, the day of the earthquake was a day that the medical students and doctors had stayed home in protest – a political action that, ironically, saved many of their lives. The nurses and nursing students, who placed patient care and learning ahead of politics, were not so lucky. As André would later learn, an entire class of nursing students and their instructors perished inside the nursing school.

As foreign policy projects that focused on the cities forced the descendants of the Revolution to abandon their birthright by the hundreds of thousands, some crossed the border into the Dominican Republic. Others crammed into wooden sailboats, hoping to make it to the Bahamas, Jamaica, or if miraculously possible, to Miami. However, most found their way to Port-au-Prince and squatted on seemingly uninhabitable land – the mudflats by the port or the almost vertical "bidonville" on the hillsides flanking Rue Pan Americain. André had taken these "bidonville" as a fact of life during his trips to his home in Bourdon. They had been built with concrete blocks one at a time by their inhabitants. Now they were gone, leaving the hillsides bare and filling the ravine below with a huge pile of rubble. The neighborhoods around Rue Pan Americain and the slums above it were among the most densely populated in the world. Now, everywhere he looked, André saw people alone or in groups, clawing through the rubble until their fingers bled, searching for loved ones, or trying to free victims, alive or dead, pinned beneath the rubble.

The road to his home was blocked by a landslide, so André and his friends parked their truck and ascended the last three hundred yards on foot. His neighborhood was an old one, full of antique homes in "Caribbean gingerbread" style. Those homes built exclusively of wood fared fairly well, giving André hope that his family's home might have been spared. Indeed, the wooden parts of their home were still standing but the brick facade, which faced the street, had crumbled, leaving only the arches surrounding the red wooden doors standing. His sister-in-law was sitting on a remnant of the wall in front of the house – she had been outside, taking in the evening breeze when the earthquake struck. She then spent the night on the sidewalk, fearing an aftershock might bring down the rest of the house. In fact, there had been three of those terrifying aftershocks throughout the night and early morning, along with several smaller ones. André spent about an hour with his sister-in-law. He told her of the chaos and horror he had witnessed in his journey across town and then helped her decide what she would do; there were neighbors whose homes had survived and who would take her in. It would be best for her to take some food and clothes with her and wait until phone and radio service were restored. Then she could find out just how bad the damage was and when it would be safe to travel, either by car to stay with family outside the capital or, if the airport was functioning, by plane to Miami. As for André, after spending the night in an open courtyard with a group of survivors, he decided he needed to go somewhere that he might be able to do some good. Perhaps Petionville, had survived – he has always been impressed as to how solid the four-story edifice appeared to be. So, he loaded the contents of his sister-in-law's refrigerator into an "*igloo*" (Kreyol slang for a cooler) into the back of his truck, along with two cases of bottled water and some bags of rice and beans from her pantry, before setting off to find a route to Petionville.

Chapter 29
Missing in Action

Dr. Michel Dodard, another Haitian American faculty at the Miller School of Medicine, spent the night after the earthquake gathering intelligence on the damage done to his homeland. Many faculty members from the Miller School of Medicine had been engaged in Haiti since the founding of Project Medishare in 1994. They knew that if anyone could get information from the ground, it would be Michel. Cable news had surprisingly little to report. He did get through, however, to his two brothers who still lived in Haiti via the Internet. One of them lived high up on *Morne Noir* with a sweeping view of the entire capital through his binoculars. Once the sun came up, he gave Michel an accurate accounting of what he could see.

The concerned faculty gathered in a conference room in the Department of Family Medicine at seven a.m. Dr. Barth Green, the Chair of Neurosurgery and one of the founders of Project Medishare, had recruited a private jet from a wealthy patient and was planning to head down to Port-au-Prince later that day along with a trauma surgeon and two surgical residents.

"Be careful," Michel warned him. "The terminal is severely damaged and when you get there, you will have nothing to work with. The Port-au-Prince you knew is gone.

My brother tells me there is nothing standing. The National Cathedral is a pile of rubble, as is the Episcopal Cathedral with all its historic murals. The hospital and the medical school are down. The only landmarks still recognizable are the new Digicel building and the cemetery! Even the dome of the presidential palace has collapsed."

"Well, I am going down anyway," said Dr. Green. "The army is sending a helicopter from Guantanamo to secure the airport and identify a safe landing area – there are plenty of Americans who need to be evacuated, so making the airport functional right away is a priority."

"What about Marie and our workers in Thomonde?" someone from the group asked.

I spoke with her this morning," responded Dr. Green. "Ironically, the phone service is better in the Central Plateau than it is in the capital. She and our team are fine. There is minor damage to our clinic in Marmont. She has a group of nursing students with her who are in a near panic. However, she will be loading them into our trucks along with as many of our community health workers as possible and will meet me at the airport."

"What about André?" another faculty member inquired.

"Oh, he's the one person you don't have to worry about. He had an important meeting at The Residency Program in Cap Haitian this morning, so he is up there, safe and sound!"

Chapter 30
Miss Marie

Now that was curious, thought Marie Chery, Medishare's Country Director, as she was about to sit down for dinner after a long day at one of Medishare's mobile clinics. Then, after a brief pause to reflect, she decided yes, it had to be an earthquake. The ground moved under her feet. Nothing as violent as she would later learn had befallen Port-au-Prince – she was more than 100 km and two mountain ranges from the epicenter. However, the trees did sway, as did the buildings that made up The Medishare complex in Thomonde; a guest house, kitchen, office, and a large tournelle (a round, open but covered space used for common meals and meetings). She had hoped for a brief respite before the evening's debriefing with the small group of University of Miami nursing students, finishing their dinner under the tournelle, about twenty yards away. These students were halfway through a one-week international nursing experience under Marie's supervision. In rural Haiti, where doctors are a rarity, nurses are the backbone of the healthcare delivery system. Marie led a team of Haitian nurses, pharmacists, chauffeurs, and community health workers that provided primary care and preventative services to more than one hundred thousand people spread out in isolated hamlets and solitary farms in the mountainous terrain that defines the southern edge of Haiti's Central Plateau. To witness Marie and her team at work was inspirational to the Miami students, as well as empowering – saving lives through simple interventions such as prenatal care, immunization campaigns, and nutrition programs. Over and above their clinical experience, however, they, as was true of practically all medical and nursing students who worked with Medishare, were having a life experience; discovering a world they did not know existed, the timeless world of suffering and hard work, as well as simple pleasures that shaped life in rural Haiti.

In 1996, through an improbable sequence of events, a delegation of "*notables*" (prominent citizens) from Thomonde came to Miami and invited Project Medishare to come to the commune to help with the abysmal state of health care there (see *The Zombie Curse*, pp. 169-184). At the time, Medishare was looking for a place no other N.G.O. had yet claimed, to teach global health. Thomonde, isolated in a gigantic volcanic caldera, with dozens of remote communities scattered in hills and valleys represented both the challenge and opportunity Medishare had been looking for. To fulfil its promise, however, the program there would need a leader.

At the time, Marie was working at the University of Miami as a research nurse. She had heard of Project Medishare and decided to volunteer and to travel to Thomonde with one of the student trips. Although she never admitted it, perhaps she was skeptical that a group of non-Haitians, visiting episodically, could ever accomplish anything meaningful in a country so impoverished, so exotic, and so unique in its history and culture.

To her surprise, Marie discovered in the Central Plateau a way she could fulfil her lifelong dream of giving back to the country she so loved. When a Miami foundation, the Green

Family Foundation, gave Medishare the funds to set up a community health program in the Central Plateau in 1999, Marie gave up her job and comfortable life in Miami for the rewards and challenges of running a health program in rural Haiti. At that time, there was no electricity and no running water in Thomonde. When she began, the ride from Port-au-Prince took six hours, a journey of 92 kilometers, on arguably the world's worst road!

For most of the seven years that followed, the rewards of managing the project far exceeded the challenges. The population Medishare cared for grew from thirty-five thousand to one hundred thousand patients, as requested by the Ministry of Health, by taking on two districts outside the Commune of Thomonde- Marmontjust to the north and Casse – La Hoye on the Dominican border. Immunization rates soared while the number of cases of AIDS and tuberculosis plummeted. In less than a decade, childhood mortality was cut in half, from 1 in 5 to 1 in 10. Most of the credit, it was generally conceded, for those successes was owed to Marie.

The past year had been difficult, however. Marie locked horns with a local politician who wanted to control her program, forcing her to fire unproductive employees who believed they were protected as his political protégés. Demonstrations in front of the Medishare compound were coupled with nighttime surreptitious graffiti attacks declaring "*au bas, Miss Marie!*" (Down with Miss Marie!). These political actions were soon followed by death threats. In the end, the people, however, stayed with Marie, as one could visibly see her successes throughout Thomonde. Most of its citizens saw through the game the politician was playing and tired of his abuse of power. Marie was the first person to stand up to him and his most outrageous abuse – the use of his position to exploit the girls and young women of the commune.

Later that evening, a call to Medishare, Miami, confirmed Marie's suspicions – a major earthquake had struck, leveling the capital. Dr. Green would be coming down with a small surgical team the following day and would need her and her staff's help in setting up a field hospital. Her priority, however, was to evacuate the nursing students. She gathered them under the tournelle to apprise them of the situation.

"The runway at the airport is intact," she told the understandably anxious students, many of whom had already been in touch with their parents or friends in Miami via cell phone. "U.N. troops have secured the perimeter and the U.S. Army will begin evacuating U.S. citizens tomorrow morning. We'll have an early breakfast and leave just after sunrise. Don't worry, we have the best drivers in Haiti, so we will be sure to get you home. Why don't you all start packing your bags, one less thing to do in the morning…"

After the nursing students left, Marie called her Chief of Security, Riche, who lived across the street from the compound. She asked him to gather the staff who lived nearby for a briefing. Although Marie supervised over hundred employees, most lived in remote, isolated villages in the mountains and valleys surrounding Thomonde. Only about twenty – the drivers, her nursing and pharmacy staff, and a few community health workers – lived close enough to rally on short notice.

Marie paced back and forth on the cement path from the entry gate to her room in the back of the compound, while she waited for her staff to arrive. She tried calling her cook and housekeeper in her apartment in Port-au-Prince – Medishare let her keep an apartment in the capital to escape the spartan conditions of the Plateau on weekends. She loved her cook and housekeeper as if they were sisters. The phone rang once and went directly to an automated message. Marie hung up before the message finished; she suspected there would be no service but had hoped against hope for a small miracle.

"We head for Port-au-Prince at first light," she told her staff. "Drivers, make sure the trucks are filled with diesel before we leave; we may not be able to get gas in Port-au-Prince for days, if not weeks. Nanette (her pharmacist), we will need to take with us as much antibiotics, pain medicine, and *sewom* (oral rehydration therapy packets) as we can carry. Also, we'll need sutures, gauze pads, adhesive tape, and latex gloves. Medishare Miami will be flying in planes with doctors and nurses, but they all need our help. Cooks, we'll need bags of rice and beans and lots of bottles of water. Everyone, prepare yourself; you'll need to be strong. I'm told it's very, very bad."

The staff dispersed quietly to begin preparations. Marie grabbed a flashlight from her bedroom and started surveying the buildings of the compound for damage. Good news there; no damage! Then she headed off with Riche and Nanette to Marmont, about a half hour drive, to pick up medicines and look for damage at Medishare's facilities there.

The Maternity Center, recently built thanks to the generosity of the family of one of the Miami medical students, was unharmed. The clinic, built by the Ministry of Health decades ago was another story, however – essentially split in two by a large crack right through the foundation.

"I don't know where we'll ever find the money to rebuild

this," Marie murmured to herself. The clinic served twenty-five thousand people, usually seeing about two hundred patients on any given day. The damage to the clinic was a huge problem – repairing it would be one more mountain to climb after a series of mountains she had already scaled to make Medishare's program in the Central Plateau succeed. Little did she know then of the even larger mountains that lay ahead.

Marie could not sleep that night, compulsively calling the cell phone of her cook and housekeeper, futilely hoping they would answer. She packed her suitcase, showered and dressed well before dawn, then went over to the Medishare headquarters to organize everyone for the days ahead. The drivers strapped containers with sutures and medicines to the tops of their trucks. The cooks not only had to prepare breakfast for the departing students and staff but also pack coolers with enough food and water for several days. She instructed the staff that remained behind to do the best they could with their previously scheduled assignments – a mobile clinic in Savanette had been scheduled for that day. The drivers would drop health workers off there before the convoy departed for Port-au-Prince. The nurse and receptionist at the clinic in Marmont were instructed to direct patients across the street to the Maternity Center – it would have to serve double duty for the foreseeable future.

Marie sat in the front passenger seat of the lead truck. In the back seats were two nurses, the pharmacist, and two community health workers, who would serve as all-purpose helpers. Everything was surreally normal for the first ten km or so as they descended National Road 3. It could have been any day in the timeless Central Plateau – children in uniforms heading to school, women carrying buckets of water on their heads back to their homes or leading their burros loaded with produce, off to the market. When they passed through Cange, however, the small village that served as the home of the hospital established by Partners in Health, it became abundantly clear that this was no ordinary day; only fifteen hours after the earthquake, throngs of injured had somehow found a way to make the seventy-five kilometer journey from the capitol to the one hospital people knew they could count on to be open for care. People clamored around the emergency room entrance, pleading they or their loved ones needed to be seen next, while those less ill backed up outside of shouting distance, laying on mats by the side of the road, begging passersby for food or water. For the rest of the journey, Marie's caravan weaved in and out of a constant stream of traffic – pedestrians, *tap-taps* and trucks inching their way towards Cange.

The convoy descended from Cange, following the shoreline of *Lac Péligre* (Danger Lake), traversed the Artibonite valley and ascended *Mont Kabrit* (Goat Mountain), the last mountain before the plain that led to Port-au-Prince. As they crested Mont Kabrit and began their descent – still around twenty-five km from the capital – Marie gasped at what she saw. She had made this trip at least once a week for years and assumed that her eyes would be greeted by the same panorama they had always seen from that vantage; a city nestled at the base of a far mountain range to the south and an azure bay to the west. Instead, all she could see was a chalky grey cloud obscuring all the usual landmarks, with a tail of dust, almost like a comet's, blown by the Tradewinds over the bay.

There were few signs of damage as the convoy passed

through the city of Croix de Bouquets. The bus depot there, however, was mobbed with people – some seemingly able-bodied and some clearly injured, as witnessed by their slings, bandages, and makeshift crutches. All were vying for spots on the *tap-taps* (taxi cabs) heading north.

The convoy was forced to halt several hundred yards from the airport, as thousands of people clamored for entry. The U.S. Army had cordoned off the perimeter and established several entry points, with armed guards and barricades. Megaphones, barely audible over the din, blared repeatedly in English and Kreyol, "U.S. citizens only may enter here."

Marie instructed the nursing students to hold their passports over their heads and follow her. At the head of the crowd, she announced loudly in Kreyol, "Volunteer nurses! We must let them go home!" Miraculously, for a few moments the din subsided and a path through the crowd appeared leading to a checkpoint, Marie spoke with the guards who explained to the nurses how they would be evacuated and where they should wait on the tarmac until the cargo planes from Guantanamo arrived. "Don't linger in the terminal," a guard cautioned, "it's not safe!"

For Marie, who had passed through the airport so many times, the scene they confronted defied belief. The place was so empty that the footsteps of her entourage echoed from room to room. Single file, they snaked around puddles and fallen ceiling tiles (the sprinkler system had gone off during the quake).

Outside on the tarmac, abandoned Air Canada and American Airlines jets were parked slightly to the east. Marie was relieved to see two C-130 cargo planes already idling to the west. They weren't big enough by themselves to evacuate the already thousands of US citizens that made their way to the airport, most of whom were sitting in the shade of one of the airplane hangars. These evacuees were mostly White, many with matching t-shirts identifying their missionary groups or N.G.O.s, with faces that expressed extreme anxiety, despite the encouraging words of their guards that they would soon be back home in the United States. It was reassuring to Marie, nonetheless, that the runways were functioning.

Marie hugged each of the nurses and received, in turn, their grateful tears and thanks. "You will be fine now," she told them. "The army is here in force and the runways survived intact. I must leave you now to prepare for Dr. Green and his team."

The army would not let her bring her team on to the tarmac, despite her protestations that they needed to rendezvous with a medical relief team that she was told was at the far end of the runway. Her team was Haitian, she was told, and therefore not allowed inside. Instead, she was told to take them around to the adjacent U.N. camp, which had become the makeshift repository for the severely injured.

Chapter 31
The Orphanage

André's hope that he could find a hospital or clinic where he could work in Petionville was based on its history. It and the hills behind it were the traditional home of Port-au-Prince's elite. It sat on a rise about five hundred meters above the port – a site chosen for its cool breezes and fewer pests (mosquitoes are said not to be able to fly above 350 meters). The buildings there were older and sturdier than other neighborhoods and many of them had survived prior earthquakes, as well as the annual onslaught of hurricanes and tropical storms. In fact, he became cautiously optimistic as he ascended Rue Pan Americain – the damage seemed spottier and the terrain more recognizable. That optimism was tempered, however, when he passed the Hotel Montana. Once Haiti's most popular hotel, the quake had reduced it to a pile of rubble. André continued onward. Surely God would spare Hospice Pere Damien – a hospital founded by a Catholic priest to care for Haiti's sickest children. His hopes, however, were shattered when he arrived at the location where the hospital used to be; five stories of concrete now imploded upon itself, the only collapsed building within sight, as if singled out for destruction by the forces of evil. Fortunately, the patients and staff had moved to a new location in Tabarre a few months before. He parked his car a few blocks away and walked to the hospital grounds, hoping he might be able to help some survivors. Sadly, however, he could find none – just families climbing on the rubble, looking for corpses and a row of about fifty dead children lined neatly in front of the rubble, waiting for their families to claim them.

It was late afternoon and André had traced a great arc from the Visa Lodge, through downtown Port-au-Prince, over to his family's homes in Bourdon and Paco and up to Petionville. Perhaps it would be best to return to the Visa Lodge, he thought. It was close to the airport, which he hoped would re-open soon, so that he could fly home. The most direct route from Petionville would be to descend Rue Delmas, then through some side streets he hoped to find that were passable.

André made it to upper Delmas without difficulty and started to descend the road towards the airport, stopping to visit an aunt along the way. Normally, one of Port-au-Prince's busiest thoroughfares, that morning it was deserted. The usually bustling shops housed in two or three story buildings were crushed by the weight of their upper stories – one building after another "pancaked." The sidewalks, normally bustling with pedestrians, schoolchildren, and vendors, were empty, except for the occasional line of corpses, and one block with an edifice, opposite his aunt's house, that miraculously escaped destruction, that was bustling with throngs of people gathered in front of its iron gate.

It was an orphanage that André knew as well-staffed by a small contingency of nuns trained as nurses from The Sisters of Mercy. It had an infirmary and dispensary.

Perhaps I could be useful here, he thought. "I am a doctor!" he told the Director as he entered the gate, "and I have some medicine and supplies in my truck."

"Then please come in," the Director serenely responded.

"We have many injured here." She then addressed the crowd, "Please let the good doctor in." Instantly, the clamoring crowd hushed and those in front of the gate pushed to either side. Some formed a work detail to help André unload the medicines and supplies from his truck.

The orphanage had an emergency generator and a bank of batteries to assure electrical power. About twenty injured patients were inside, as well as five in the courtyard, some on beds previously occupied by orphans, some on school benches placed side by side and others stretched out on the floor. The good sisters had been washing wounds with soap and water and splinting obviously mangled limbs with broken furniture but lacked sutures and gauze. To have a doctor arrive with supplies seemed truly a miracle. They organized themselves to make rounds with André, eager to get his opinion on those that they considered most severely injured. Even though it was just a day since the quake, there were several patients who already showed early signs of gangrene.

They will need amputations to save their lives, André thought. *If only we had anesthesia ...*

Chapter 32
A Dialogue

André had no time to sleep that night – the nuns, who were also nurses, rounded on each patient, recording their vital signs and injuries on a piece of paper, which they taped to each patient to serve as a makeshift "*dosier.*" André offered words of encouragement to each patient while the nuns offered benedictions. The patients, in turn, (at least those able to talk) both thanked and blessed the team that was ministering to them. Some, with major head trauma, were clearly not going to make it. André asked the nurses to carry them and their cots to a small room in the back of the orphanage. There, they washed them and dressed them in the least tattered clothes they could find, in anticipation that they would be prepared for a proper burial.

While the nuns tended the dying, André returned to his makeshift ward – suturing the wounds of patients with lacerations and setting simple fractures. Most of these fractures were "greenstick" – the kind that happens when you hold your hand above your head to deflect heavy falling objects. "A moment of pain," he would warn each patient, followed by a downward pull on the wrist and a straightening by sight of the forearm. To keep the fracture set, he would splint the limb using tape and slats of wood rescued from broken chairs.

What worried him the most, however, were the small group of patients with compound fractures – fractures in which the completely broken bone perforated the skin. These patients would die of shock or gangrene if not operated on soon.

One of the patients with a compound fracture was it twenty one-year-old youth. It was four in the morning and this boy was singing hymns to himself, bobbing his head back and forth in a rhythmic trance. André peeled back the sheet covering the lower half of his right arm. The lower half of his right leg and foot lay at a right angle to the rest of his leg. Green pus stained his gauze dressing, which was already smelling of gangrene. One small silver lining – if only he could operate, he could save his knee, which would make it much easier for him to walk again. The poor boy was at a crossroads, André thought. He may die, or he may never be able to work again – he had recently completed training as an electrician. If he can't walk, he can't work – he will be forced to survive by begging on the church steps. André pulled up a chair, sat down, leaned forward, and clasped his hands between his legs.

"What's your name?" André asked softly.

"Nelson," the youth replied.

"What happened to you?"

"I was playing *futbol* in the church courtyard across the street when the church wall fell on me. All my friends died, but I was at the edge of the field and managed to pull myself free. A policeman carried me here…"

"Where are your parents?"

"I only have a father. He drives a *tap-tap*. I don't know where he is, and he doesn't know where I am."

"Your arm is bad. I'm not sure it can be saved…" In fact, André knew his arm could not be saved. The real question was could his life be saved?

"Well, whatever God wants. May His will be done."

"You may not be able to play football again."

"Whatever God wants. One way or the other, good will come of it. What is it like out there?"

"Are you going to school?" André didn't want to talk about the earthquake.

"Yes, I come here to the orphanage school!"

"Are you a good student?"

"Yes! I hope to be a doctor or a priest when I grow up!"

"There are similarities in both jobs," said André, with an ironic smile.

Since the first tremors of the quake, André had been running on adrenaline. There was probably a small opportunity to lie down for an hour or two, but he was too alert, too excited. Instead, he chose to stay and continue his dialogue with Nelson, if only to distract him from the pain. He admired the boy's courage and stamina as he watched the stain of pus on his gauze dressing expand and as the stench of decaying flesh grew stronger. Noting the beads of perspiration forming on his forehead, André could not be sure how much lucid time Nelson had left.

Chapter 33
Prayers Are Answered

As the sun rose the following morning, the nuns led their patients in prayer and singing hymns. Two of the nuns went to the back room, washed the dead, wrapped them in sheets with their faces exposed and took them outside to take their place beside the other dead. A third nun assumed the post of sentry at the front gate, allowing in families of the patients inside. They brought them whatever food they could scavenge and helped the patients with their morning ablutions.

André was still sitting with Nelson, encouraging him to be strong, when the triage nurse approached him from behind and tapped him on the shoulder. "Dr. Vulcain, our prayers have been answered!" André turned to see a man and woman in surgical scrubs and caps.

"We're the anesthesiologist and nurse anesthetist from the University Hospital. We heard you were here. We salvaged some local anesthetics from Central Supply, along with some sterile drapes and I.V. fluids."

"Lidocaine!" André exclaimed, as he bolted upright out of his chair. "Now we can operate!"

Later, he confessed that in the chaos, sleep deprivation and excitement of the moment, he could not recall the names of these good Samaritans, but they immediately set up a makeshift operating room in a room on the south side of the orphanage – one with sunlight shining through the windows. André commandeered a toolkit from his aunt's house and sterilized his instruments in a pot of boiling water over a charcoal stove. In an hour, they were ready to go. Nelson was their first patient.

They performed three operations that day and, in the evening, André finally allowed himself to relax. The nuns brought him food and the anesthesiologist brought him news; it had been a massive earthquake with most of Port-au-Prince and the suburbs to the south, extending all the way to Leogane (André's hometown) destroyed. Millions were homeless and no one was sure how many were dead. However, the airport runway was intact, and the US Army was coming in to assist the United Nations in re-establishing order. Afraid to return to their homes, even if their home survived, most survivors were sleeping out of doors. Fortunately, it had not rained. Finally, the University of Miami had somehow managed to set up a field hospital at the U.N. Camp next to the airport.

Chapter 34
Lost and Found

By day three post-quake, the University of Miami Miller School of Medicine had established a "war room" command center in a large conference room on campus to coordinate its relief efforts in Haiti. It had already established a makeshift field hospital within the United Nations compound next to the airport, and organized private jets lent by wealthy South Floridians into a rotation of three flights per day, bringing in personnel, medicine, equipment, and supplies.

Faculty volunteers and administrators from both the medical school and its teaching hospitals, Jackson Memorial Hospital, and the Miami Veterans Administration Medical Center, gathered at seven a.m. each morning. Morning Report began with a clinical de-briefing by satellite phone with one of the surgeons at the field hospital. Day four's debriefing was led by Dr. Green.

"It's hell down here! We already have two hundred critically ill patients, and more are arriving by the hour. We turned a large cargo container into a makeshift morgue. We need large plastic bags to put amputated limbs into. We need more sterile surgical trays and Ketamine! What's taking you so long for the morphine?"

"It's coming down on today's plane," one of the administrators volunteered. "We had some paperwork to do;

it's a controlled substance, you know, you can't just pluck it off the shelf."

"Yeah, tell that to our amputees!" was Dr. Green's retort.

The clinical debriefing was followed by a situation report led by Dr. Dodard.

"Estimates of the dead are climbing daily – the latest is over one hundred thousand people, but no one knows for sure. Getting around the city is impossible; all the roads are filled with debris. The army has started evacuation flights but only for U.S. citizens. There is severe damage to the General Hospital. The medical and nursing schools are gone. The Red Cross has started to distribute food and water by helicopter, but they are afraid to land, so they are just dropping supplies out of their doors. There is no crowd control, so there's panic and disappointment whenever they do this. People are clawing through the rubble with their bare hands, looking for survivors, extracting the dead, but also scavenging for food and water. The U.N. Command has issued a shoot to kill order to their patrols for looters. It's very sad. They aren't really looters they are shooting, just survivors searching for food."

After a brief pause, he continued in the solemn voice. "Also, I must report we are missing one of our own. Dr. André Vulcain was supposed to be in Cap Haitian for a meeting, but he never made it there. His family is frantic. If those of you on the ground have any news of his whereabouts, please let us know immediately…"

By the morning of the fourth day, the orphanage was quiet and organized. André was upbeat as he rounded on his patients. None of the amputees were febrile and the nurses saw no signs of pus or bleeding as they changed their dressings. Nelson was doing particularly well, already sitting up in bed and learning how to transfer to a chair and stand up on crutches. After finishing rounds and dressing changes, André spoke to the anesthesiologist.

"I've done all I can do here, I'll leave you in charge. I'm going down to the airport to see if the rumors about the University of Miami and a field hospital are true."

The crowd outside the gate knew André was the doctor who treated their loved ones and neighbors inside, so they separated to let him depart, many of them offering benedictions as he passed. His truck was covered with four days' worth of chalk dust, but after two squirts of his wiper fluid he set down Rue Delmas to find his way to the airport. Delmas, usually a major thoroughfare, was now passable, although its curb sides were littered with abandoned cars, trucks, and *tap-taps*.

House after house had "pancaked" and the lines of neatly arranged corpses on the sidewalk had grown exponentially since he first arrived. Four days after the quake, survivors were still climbing through the rubble, searching for loved ones alive or dead and scavenging for food and water. People had set up makeshift tents using bed sheets, clotheslines and splintered boards as struts and pegs.

On the airport road, the damage was less obvious, but everywhere, the makeshift tents continued. Powerful aftershocks had convinced the people that it was unsafe to return to their houses. The only other vehicles on the road were United Nations Humvees, patrolling for "looters." As he approached the airport, he noticed tent cities were already being set up by the Red Cross – their locations dictated more for the convenience of the Red Cross than the needs of the people. He went directly to the U.N. compound, as he had heard that that was where the University of Miami had set up its field hospital. The U.N. soldiers had set up a perimeter, however, sealing off the entrance to the horde of Haitians seeking entry, hoping it would be a source of food, shelter, and medical care. Unable to fight his way through the crowd, André proceeded on foot to the airport about three hundred yards down the road.

The perimeter of the airport entry was maintained by the U.S. Army, not the United Nations. When André waved his documents to a soldier barked at him, calling him to come forward. After he explained that he was a doctor with the University of Miami, the soldier escorted him through the airport, across the tarmac and over to the U.N. compound. As he emerged from the terminal onto the tarmac, he noticed a large crowd of mostly white people to the left, sitting in the shade of an abandoned building. André assumed they were U.S. citizens waiting to be evacuated. Nearby were several C-130s. He followed the soldier to the right, past a large jet with Hebrew letters on the tail (the Israeli Rapid Response Team) to the end of the tarmac, through a check-point, across a small field, another checkpoint, and finally into the U.N. compound itself. No need to search for the U.N. "field hospital" – two canopies set up side by side in what had once been a grassy courtyard. All he needed to do was follow the soldiers carrying in the wounded on stretchers. Each canopy covered hundreds of cots, each one with a patient, often accompanied by families. Intravenous lines were suspended from clothes lines that crisscrossed the tents like spiderwebs. Scores of doctors and nurses moved tactfully through the rows of cots, sometimes stopping to check the notes pinned to the patient's bed clothes, sometimes pushing medicines into their I.V. lines.

It was also easy to find Marie, with her signature close-cropped orange-tinted hair and scrubs with a Project

Medishare logo emblazoned on the back. She was in the middle of changing a dressing as André approached. When he called her name, she looked up, gasped, stood up, and gave him a scissors hug, not wanting to violate the sterility of her latex gloves.

"We were so worried about you! Just let me finish this dressing change and we'll have time to talk!"

After she finished and disposed of the old gauze and her gloves, Marie led André over to the makeshift morgue. "It's the only place quiet enough to have a conversation!" she explained.

André told Marie of his decision not to fly to Cap Haitian on the afternoon of the earthquake, his night at the Visa Lodge, his sojourn through the city, and his work at the orphanage in Delmas. He was now ready to pitch in at the field hospital if he was needed.

"No, André, we've got plenty of help here. Dr. Green and Dr. Ginsberg (a U.M. trauma surgeon) are here and we have three planes – private jets – coming in every day since the day after the earthquake. They bring in ten to twelve volunteers each. Frankly, it's a bit overwhelming, as the United Nations has not been particularly welcoming – we are sleeping on the grass and on top of cardboard mats and we've had to fly in our own food and water. No, you should go home. Babette is so worried. I will call her on our satellite phone as soon as we have a break."

They hugged again and André left the U.N. compound, heading over to what he thought were the evacuation planes on the far end of the tarmac. Indeed, the army had several tables set up and several lines had formed in front of the soldiers, who had stacks of forms that needed to be completed to qualify for evacuation. "Please keep your documents handy," the soldiers patrolling the lines kept repeating. "Only U.S. citizens and residents are being allowed on these planes. You must be able to prove your U.S. citizenship or residency!"

André picked a line and after several minutes, advanced to the front of it. The soldier sitting there checked his passport and handed him two forms to complete. One was the standard Customs form, the other was more earthquake-specific. How long had he been in the country prior to the quake, had he been injured, who should be notified in case of an emergency. The soldier ripped off a stop at the bottom of the second form.

"This will serve as your boarding pass," he explained. "We board first come first serve, and as you can see from your number, there are a lot of people ahead of you. You'll probably be here for three days. We'll do our best to get food and water to you."

Waiting on the tarmac for three days seemed foolish to André, so he walked over to the Red Cross staging area and sought out the person in charge. "I'm a doctor," he explained. "Is there any place you could use me for three days but get me back here in time for my return flight home?"

"Well, this chopper is heading out to Leogane," the volunteer responded. "We are setting up a MASH unit there, but our doctors won't arrive for a couple of days. It's bad out there – the entire town has been flattened. It's the closest town to the quake's epicenter, you know."

Leogane. André's heart sank in his chest. "That's my hometown! I have a truck and can get medical supplies. I'll head out there!"

Chapter 35
The MASH Unit

The thirty-minute helicopter ride from the airport to Leogane left André in awe of the scope of destruction, not only to Port-au-Prince, but for the entire fifty km to his hometown, Leogane. None of the destruction he had seen in the first few days (and it was enormous!) compared to that of Carrefour, the capital's largest suburb, now entirely reduced to a giant pile of rubble.

Leogane, although a much smaller city, fared no better. In colonial times, it was a prosperous port that served the lucrative sugar plantations that lined the coastal plain on the north side of Haiti's southern peninsula. Over the centuries, erosion from the deforested mountains behind the city filled in the harbor. The population dwindled even as the town became the support center for a regional hospital, Hopital Ste. Croix. Owned by the Episcopal Church and financed by the American Presbyterian Church, the hospital had fallen upon hard times, even before the earthquake. A clogged sewer line had forced the closing of the inpatient services, leaving only a freestanding emergency room and outpatient clinic. Now, even these structures were gone. In fact, everything in Leogane was gone. Without familiar, recognizable structures, André was completely disoriented. While the Red Cross unloaded the helicopter and cleared away the rubble to set up a MASH unit, he searched in vain for his grandparents' house. Four days after the quake, as he combed the streets of his ancestral home, most people were still standing in a state of shock. Those who had shaken off the shock were either gathering in makeshift congregations in open spaces, hands held to the sky, singing hymns and praying, or waiting patiently at the Red Cross Distribution Center for MREs and bottled water to be unloaded.

For the next three days, André tended to the injured of Leogane. The first day was the most difficult, as he was the only physician in the MASH unit. His priority was triage – identifying those critically ill patients who would need to be airlifted to Port-au-Prince. André went from cot to cot, examining each patient and instructing the nurses as to which patients needed I.V.s, pain medicines or antibiotics. Four days after the quake meant that it was too late for sutures; small wounds would need to close themselves, while wounds to the bone would require amputation of the affected limb. All received tetanus shots to prevent the dreaded complication of lockjaw, which would have been a death sentence under these circumstances.

Fortunately, the choppers had brought plenty of supplies with them and were making round trips for more every hour. Those patients who had already developed gangrene, those with spinal cord injuries, those in shock from hemorrhage, and those with skull fractures or crushed pelvises were removed to a tent near the makeshift heliport, to await being airlifted to hospitals in Port-au-Prince. André gave words of encouragement to these patients as he sent them on their way.

What fortitude, he thought, *to suffer in silence for four days, clinging to their belief that God will deliver them from this evil.*

After completing triage rounds, André began cleaning and dressing wounds and setting simple fractures. He and the nurses worked through the night. When relief arrived the following morning, the new Red Cross volunteers found a well-organized Field Hospital / MASH unit.

There was still plenty to do the following day. Each patient needed to be signed off to the relief doctors and new patients in need of triage continued to arrive from the surrounding countryside, frequently carried on the backs of family members and neighbors. The relief doctors could not speak Kreyol, so André also served as a translator. André made rounds early on the morning of his third day in Leogane. He then thanked the nurses who had helped him, as well as the relief workers, bade farewell to his patients, then headed to his truck for a ride back to the airport.

Chapter 36
Homeward Bound

From the road, there appeared to have been little improvement in Carrefour and the neighborhoods south and east of the capital. Streets were still impossible to navigate, people were still meandering on foot, snaking their way to relief centers and water stations. As he passed by the presidential palace, André noticed that a large encampment of tents had been set up in Champs Mars, the park that extended out from the government buildings. That panoramic view – the partially collapsed presidential palace, the destroyed ministries, the tens of thousands of people suddenly homeless seared into André's consciousness the enormity of the disaster. Would his beloved Haiti ever recover?

Andre pulled into the Red Cross staging area on the airport tarmac. André thanked the pilots and, passport, customs form, and makeshift boarding pass in hand, headed towards the C-130 transport planes that he hoped would take him home. He once again passed through the lines to prove his residency and then waited with others until the plane was ready to board.

The plane had been reconfigured with makeshift jump sheets to maximize the number of people being evacuated. André buckled his seatbelt as the plane taxied down the runway. He made polite conversation with the passengers on either side for a few minutes, then sighed deeply – sigh of relief that he was finally going home but also a sigh of sorrow for Haiti.

Exhausted and sleep-deprived, André began to drift into slumber soon after takeoff, when the pilot's voice came over the intercom. "The trip to Chicago should take four hours. Conditions on the ground are 18 degrees and light snow."

Chicago? André thought incredulously. He naturally assumed they would be flying to Miami. However, the plane had been drafted for evacuation from a military base near Chicago and that would be their returning destination. André would need to take a commercial flight from Chicago to Miami. And to think he had given his winter coat to his brother! He was forced to say home for a month until commercial flights resumed. As soon as he could, however, he resumed his routine of monthly trips to Cap Haitian to nurture and lead the Family Medicine Residency program there.

Chapter 37
Muddy Waters

Marie's cell phone rang incessantly, starting shortly after sunrise on Oct 19 2010, ten months after the earthquake. The calls came from her nursing colleagues in Cange, Mirebalais, and Deschapelles. Scores of people were found dead by the side of the road that paralleled the Artibonite River. The Artibonite, Haiti's longest river, ran from just above Mirebalais to the coastal plain near the cities of St. Marc and Gonaives. It flowed swiftly near its source, the dam at Lac Péligre, then slowed and flooded hundreds of rice paddies near its delta. The people who lived nearby drank from it, bathed, and washed their clothes in it. It was the perfect set-up for a water-borne epidemic. The dead were found in brown puddles of diarrhea. They were trying to reach the Albert Schweitzer Hospital in Deschapelles. That day, the hospital was overwhelmed with over four hundred patients with fulminant diarrhea. Most were in shock when they arrived and most died by the end of the day, after the hospital ran out of I.V. fluids.

"Could this be cholera?" Marie asked, after describing the symptoms to the Medishare doctors she worked with in Miami.

"Clinically, it sounds like it," answered André Vulcain. "But we have not seen a case since cholera was eradicated in Haiti in 1976. Where could it have come from?"

"We think it's from the U.N. camp near Mirebalais," answered Marie. "Clearly, the Artibonite is contaminated and the UN camp there is located directly on a stream that feeds into it."

Marie was not alone in her suspicions of the U.N. camp. Almost all Haitian doctors and nurses shared her view. The U.N. forces were sent to Haiti in 1994, ostensibly to maintain order after the restoration to power of President Aristide. Their mandate was renewed every two years by each successive government, if for no other reason that they infused a significant amount of money into the Haitian economy. They were extremely unpopular, however, with the people for a variety of reasons; some viewed them as instruments of foreign control, particularly when they stood by and did nothing to halt the so-called "rebellion" against Aristide in 2005. Others felt the money spent on maintaining them and supporting their meaningless patrols would have been better spent in building schools and hospitals. The U.N. troops assigned to Haiti came from two countries; Brazil and Nepal. The Brazilian contingent was despised by many Haitians for their reputation of exploiting desperately poor Haitian young women and girls. The Nepalese, however, through no fault of their own, would prove to be the source of the next plague to be inflicted on the people of Haiti.

The U.N. established a large main enclave, complete with a barbed wire enclosure and guard turrets next to the airport. This was the site of the original field hospital set up by the University of Miami. They also established satellite camps throughout the countryside. From these camps, each day, they would send patrols in SUVs and Humvees into remote corners of the countryside. The camps were supported by Haitian contractors, who provided food, water, and sanitation.

By the second day of the outbreak, six hundred more patients with diarrhea overwhelmed Hopital St. Nicolas in St. Marc. By the end of the first week, over two thousand deaths have been reported, all from the Artibonite valley. Over the next weeks and months, however, because of poor sanitation and lack of medical infrastructure, cholera soon spread throughout the country. By the time it was finally brought under control, more than two hundred thousand people were affected, and nine thousand people had died. Because the outbreak occurred in the countryside, it took some time for the story to break in the international media. When it did, everyone outside of Haiti assumed this was just another curse inflicted upon the Haitians. By then, however, the Haitians were even more certain than ever that this was not the re-emergence of a latent indigenous pathogen. Pictures had emerged of latrines in the UN camp with pipes dumping raw sewage right into the stream behind it.

The U.N. denied a role in introducing cholera. The Haitians, however, had facts on their side. There had been no reports of cholera in Haiti for forty years. It is, however, endemic in Nepal. Later, French scientists investigated the issue at the request of the Haitian government. It was discovered that the strain of cholera that erupted in Haiti matched the strain present in Nepal and not the strains that have been preserved during the last outbreak in Haiti. Furthermore, a new contingent of Nepalese troops had just been deployed to the Mirebalais camp days before the outbreak. When tested, they proved to carry the same strain that was afflicting the Haitians.

Cholera is a brutally effective pathogen. In effect, it burns the intestinal lining, causing it to leak plasma faster than the patient can replace it by drinking fluids. It multiplies rapidly in this froth, contaminating the water supply and in an immunologically naive population, killing them by the thousands. Plus, the greed of the sanitation contractors and a deployment of soldiers from a cholera-endemic country, coupled with the poor sanitation and health infrastructure in rural Haiti created a perfect storm for a cholera disaster.

Chapter 38
Bull Horns and Bleach

The weeks and months following the earthquake were painful for Marie, both personally and professionally. Her apartment in Port-au-Prince – her weekend retreat from the Spartan life she lived in the Central Plateau – was destroyed. Her cook and housekeeper, who she considered family, were missing and presumed dead for over a week. They eventually turned up alive, but the time they were missing was stressful for Marie. She also grieved for her profession. The state of Haiti Nursing School, where her mother once served as director, not only completely collapsed, but took with it an entire class of student nurses and their instructors, many of whom Marie knew personally.

Making matters worse for Marie was a change in mission and vision for Medishare that occurred after the earthquake. New people were appointed to the Medishare – Miami board who were not familiar with Marie's programs in the Central Plateau. Instead, they wanted to establish a permanent trauma hospital in Port-au-Prince – an awfully expensive undertaking!

One week after the earthquake, Marie and her Haitian crew had set up four large event tents donated by the Miami Heat and transformed them into a functioning Field Hospital. However, the "spin" by the newcomers in Miami was that she was suffering from post-traumatic stress disorder and did not have the skills to manage a trauma hospital. An American hospital administrator was brought in, and Marie was sent back to the Central Plateau to manage the programs there. Tensions arose between Marie and Medishare – Miami, as scarce resources had to be competed for between the new trauma hospital in Port-au-Prince and her community health program in the Central Plateau. For nine months, Marie struggled to continue the schedule of community health programs in the remote corners of the commune, staff and manage the new Maternity Center and host the return of medical students and nursing students who came to learn global health. At its peak, nine medical, nursing, and health professions schools spent one-week rotations in Thomonde, working side-by-side with Marie's community health workers, delivering primary care and preventative services to about one hundred thousand patients. Cholera, for Marie, gave her the opportunity to put aside the post-earthquake Medishare in-fighting. She had patients in the Central Plateau dying by the thousands and she, with her nursing training in Haiti and over a decade of experience delivering community health in the Central Plateau, knew what to do about it.

She drove down to Cange to meet with Loune Viaude, her counterpart at Zanmi La Sante (Partners in Health) to put together a plan for both treatment and prevention of cholera. They decided to set up Cholera Treatment Centers all along the Artibonite River basin. Marie brought up from Port-au-Prince the four tents that had served as Medishare's field hospital after the earthquake – six months after the quake she had "mothballed" the tents in a Port-au-Prince warehouse. She sent a crew of drivers and community health workers to deploy them in a string of strategic locations along the river basin.

Zanmi La Sante provided the I.V. solutions, antibiotics, bleach, and cholera cots – an army cot with a hole cut in it so that patients would not have to get up to void their cholera fluids. Both organizations contributed their stockpiles of Oral Rehydration Therapy – packets of a formulation of sugar and salt that allowed ingested fluids to be absorbed to restore blood volume without an intravenous line, even in the face of a severely damaged intestinal lining.

By November, her four units were up and running. The major tents were complemented by smaller tents donated by the Red Cross. These smaller tents served as lodging for staff and families, as well as triage stations, central supply, and pharmacy. When the patient arrived, they and their families passed through a series of decontamination stations – stepping on bleach-soaked mats and washing with bleach-purified water – on their way to the triage stations. Those in shock or near shock were sent to the big tent for I.V. fluids. Those less ill were given Oral Rehydration Therapy.

At the same time, Marie assembled a small army of community health workers armed with bull horns and deployed them from Thomonde to each village in the Artibonite valley. Their message was simple; cholera was back in Haiti and at the first sign of diarrhea, patients should start Oral Rehydration Therapy and head for a Cholera Treatment Center. Patients could also prevent cholera by adding eight drops of bleach to every two liters of drinking water, as well as two cups of bleach in the family latrine each day. While cholera was ravaging the rest of the country, Marie's efforts, along with those of Zanmi La Sante, were starting to pay off. If patients made it to the Cholera Treatment Centers, there was a good chance they would survive. Thanks to the bull-horn rallies, they were coming into treatment earlier in the course of their illness. Even better, the number of new cases was falling off, as workers taught isolated communities to sterilize drinking water and latrines with bleach.

Many years ago, a Miami medical student named Rick Spurlock developed a great admiration for Marie during his Global Health rotations in the Central Plateau. After he finished his training, he worked as an emergency room doctor in Atlanta and organized faculty and students from Emory and Morehouse to volunteer with Medishare, as he had done earlier. Now, hearing of cholera, he raised $35,000 to build a bleach factory on the grounds of Medishare's Maternity Center in Marmont, just north of Thomonde. Bleach is easy to make – all it takes is salt and vinegar and a machine to pass electric current through the mixture. Within two weeks of receiving these funds, Marie had a bleach factory built. Large sacks of salt and jugs of vinegar were neatly stored in a back room, along with thousands of bottles of bleach lined up to be distributed by her community health workers to every community, along with lessons on how to use it. Families receiving the bleach returned the empty bottles to their community health workers, who brought them back to the factory to be cleaned and refilled. By the end of November, when the rainy season subsided, new cases were down to a handful per week and mortality approached zero. When the rainy season returned, so would cholera, Marie told her team, but at least they had a few months of respite.

Chapter 39
Theodicy Strikes Miss Marie

Each year from 2011-2014, the arrival of the rainy season brought another outbreak of cholera. Each outbreak forced Marie to divert scarce resources from her Community Health Program to the fight against cholera. To make matters worse, the post-earthquake Medishare management team in Miami reviewed her budget each year with ever-increasing scrutiny, convinced she had a secret stash of money that could be shifted to the trauma hospital in Port-au-Prince. Somehow, she managed to deal with all this, buoyed by the fact the health of the people once again began to improve.

Improvement in childhood mortality was a big part of her success. When she first arrived in the Central Plateau, one of five children died before their fifth birthday, mostly from infantile diarrhea. Now, thanks to her Community Health Program and the availability of Oral Rehydration Therapy, by 2014 that death rate had dropped to one in ten.

The new number one cause of death in children of the Central Plateau, once infantile diarrhea was controlled, was invasive pneumococcal disease, caused by a germ that causes pneumonia and meningitis. In most of the world, these diseases were prevented by vaccines, but not in Haiti. Marie was thrilled, therefore, in 2013 when it was announced that the World Health Organization's program, GAVI (Global Alliance for Vaccines and Immunizations) would finally fund an anti-pneumococcal vaccine campaign in Haiti – the last country in the Western Hemisphere to do so.

Marie and her Community Health Program had all the pieces of the puzzle in place to rapidly implement a pneumococcal vaccine program. She had an already existing supply chain for vaccines and a system for delivering them to the people by her community health workers. Under her supervision, vaccination rates had risen from essentially zero to eighty-seven percent of all children. Cases of tetanus, rubella, and measles had fallen drastically. The problem, however, lay with the government in Port-au-Prince. First there was a lack of capacity to receive and distribute the vaccines. Impending elections and a political impasse followed that put the whole campaign on hold.

On March 1 2014, Marie awoke in Thomonde with a profound but ill-defined malaise. She had worked hard the day before, staffing the pediatric station in a mobile clinic. A particularly virulent respiratory infection had been ravishing the children there. At the time, Marie failed to make the connection between these sick children and her own sense of impending doom, a sense that some serious illness was about to befall her. *I better get myself to Miami,* she thought.

There is a standing joke among the elite and professional classes in Haiti that the best health insurance is a ticket to Miami. Marie called ahead and spoke with Dr. Green, who assured her that he would have a bed waiting for her. She then called American Airlines and made reservations for herself and one of her nurses, who would accompany her. She packed a small bag, then called for a truck and driver to take her down to the airport.

When she arrived at the airport, she barely had the strength to get through the ticket counter and customs before boarding her plane. They were flight delays, and she did not arrive in Miami until the following day. The doctors who saw her initially found nothing wrong, and as so often happens under these circumstances, they ordered a lot of tests, including a CAT scan of the brain. All tests returned negative. However, by the time she arrived in her room, she was speaking incoherently.

Then disaster struck. Her heart stopped beating. The doctors and nurses resuscitated her quickly and sent her to the ICU. By then, however, it was too late. She never regained consciousness. She was, in fact, brain-dead – a second CAT scan showed her gray matter and white matter melting together.

A Gram stain of her spinal fluid, obtained by lumbar puncture, showed Gram positive organisms in pairs and chains – diagnostic of pneumococcal meningitis. She died two days later, after exposure to the germ by one of the children she had ministered to four days before. A disease that's totally preventable by vaccine available everywhere but Haiti and curable by antibiotics if they are started early.

As she descended from Thomonde on her last journey, she passed by the Partners in Health Hospital in Cange. Its founder, Dr. Paul Farmer, is an infectious disease specialist. The laboratory there is Harvard quality and the doctors there are well-trained in rapidly diagnosing and treating common infections like meningitis. If only Marie had stopped there, while she was still lucid, she would have been started on antibiotics and her life would have been spared. Ironically, as knowledgeable as she was about the quality of care provided by Partners in Health and as closely as she had worked with them through the years, she could not escape the prejudice that her best health insurance was a ticket to Miami!

Marie's funeral was held in a large Catholic Church in Miami. The church was overflowing with Marie's friends, colleagues, and co-workers, both from her days as a nurse at Jackson Memorial Hospital and her more recent work with Medishare. The Americans in attendance were, for the most part, in shock and denial. Marie had always shown such vigor, it was hard to believe she could be taken from us so swiftly. We all assumed she would be there in the Central Plateau, fighting the good fight, forever.

The Haitians in attendance had a different mindset. They were serene, peaceful, and accepting of Marie's fate as God's will. Religious Haitians aspire to sainthood. One leads a good life and hopes one will be remembered well by one's family and community. While Americans celebrate the ghosts and ghouls of Halloween, All Souls Day, Haitians celebrate the following day, All Saints Day, as their most important religious holiday of the year. If anyone had achieved sainthood, it was Marie. It was not, however, for us to question her fate. Somehow, good would come of it.

As for me, I struggled with this. As much as I try to learn from the Haitian people and emulate their worldview, it was hard to accept this Theodicy Kreyol. There seemed no way to find justice in this, no loving Divine reward for all Marie's hard work. No, her death, to me, was more like some cruel trick of *Baron Samedi,* the Vodou god of the underworld.

That's not to say that Marie's death did not produce some tangible good. Generous people from all backgrounds and walks of life in Miami contributed to her memory and rebuilt the clinic in Marmont, dedicated to her memory. A new, bigger bleach factory was built to meet the need for clean water throughout Medishare's catchment area. Mobile clinics continue in thirty-six remote locations. Pneumococcal vaccine has been added to the vaccine program. Now, more and more women are delivering at the Maternity Center, rather than at home. Student trips resumed in the summer of 2013 (although they were suspended again in 2020 for safety concerns). Marie's name is revered throughout the region. Her picture hangs in every Medishare facility. But something is missing that cannot be replaced – that uniqueness which was Marie.

2021: The Babushka Doll Assassination

Introduction

Assassination has always been in the toolkit of Haitian presidential politics. In the two hundred-plus-year history of the country, only three presidents finished their terms – the rest were either assassinated or forced into exile. In truth, Haiti has never been a true democracy, but rather an oligarchy, with ninety percent of the wealth and all the political power wielded by ten percent of the population – traditionally through patronage and control of customs. More recently, these traditional sources of revenue have been dwarfed by the influx of dollars from the Venezuelan gas subsidy, foreign aid, and drug cartel money.

In the assassination of President Moise, one can see how the art of assassination (and getting away with it!) have been perfected as an instrument of power in Haiti. This is a tale of intrigue, infighting, useful idiots, smoke screens, and red herrings. These obfuscations have made the Western media's attempts to get to the bottom of the assassination laughable. If one peels the onion or opens the Babushka Doll one doll at a time, it is not too difficult, in broad strokes, to understand what happened. As the case is ongoing, and with a real threat of retribution (even for me, now squirreled away in a remote, isolated corner of rural Virginia), this history will not use real names. Those familiar with the Haitian political landscape, however, should be able to connect the dots.

Chapter 40
The Plot Unravels

July 7 2021: A small contingent of the assassination squad burst through the bedroom door of President Jovenel Moise sometime between one and three a.m. One assassin discharged a round of semi-automatic weapons fire into the sleeping president and his wife. The president was killed immediately. The first lady, wounded in the arms and thigh, rolled off the bed and pretended to be dead. Upstairs, hearing the shots, their daughter hid in a closet. The assassins ransacked the first floor, discovering, they later claimed, suitcases and boxes containing about $45 million. The money was loaded into the SUVs of the hit squad's caravan, and the assassins descended the road toward Petionville.

The presidential estate is hidden behind a wall in the neighborhood of Pellerin on the side of the mountain behind Pétionville. The shots awoke some of the neighbors and their servants, who furtively tried to witness what was going on without making their own whereabouts known. These witnesses said the men mostly spoke Spanish. Two wore t-shirts with the letters "D.E.A." emblazoned on their backs. Curiously, the lights of the compound were off and there were no presidential guards present.

The leader of the assassins became concerned when he noticed that the official of the Haitian government who had accompanied them to the estate, gave the kill order, and was to escort them down to the presidential palace was nowhere to be found. The plan was for them to seek protection in the presidential palace until a new president was sworn in. That plan soon dissolved into chaos, as the assassins found the road blocked by the Haitian National Police. A gunfight erupted, with the assassins taking flight on foot or seeking cover in abandoned buildings. By the following morning, three assassins were dead, twenty-eight captured and five still at large. The captured squad was mostly from Colombia, with two Haitian Americans who claimed their only purpose was to serve as translators.

The Colombians initially claimed that the presidential guard had killed the president – that they were there only to serve a warrant, charging him with corruption, and that he was already dead when they arrived at the compound. However, faced with overwhelming evidence and the possibility of a life sentence in a Haitian prison, they ultimately confessed. The five who evaded capture were never found. Neither were the suitcases and boxes of money.

Chapter 41
The Unusual Suspects

The day after the assassination, Haitian authorities announced that the plot to kill the president was carried out by well-trained and well-armed Colombian mercenaries, most of whom were in custody and being interrogated by the Haitian National Police. The Colombians, through their lawyers, told a different story. They claimed they were originally hired by a U.S. based security firm to protect prominent citizens in a time of increasing anarchy and political turmoil in Haiti. They also claimed that they went to the presidential estate solely to serve a warrant charging the president with corruption. In fact, a copy of that warrant was actually produced by their lawyers and is being held by the police as evidence.

When they arrived at the compound, there were no guards. The president was already dead, they claimed. The roadblock and ambush by the police as they left the estate was evidence, according to them, they were set up, most likely by the police themselves. Indeed, the Haitian National Police are notoriously corrupt and the fact that there were no guards at the president's home at the time of the assassination gave credence to their story.

Despite these details, no clear mastermind was identified. The Colombians said they were recruited by a South Florida security firm and that investors from South Florida financed their mission. When interrogated, the investment group claimed they were approached by a Haitian American doctor who needed security to assume the presidency. He had a plan to rebuild Haiti by investing in infrastructure (after he retained a portion of the profits, of course). The international media soon latched on to this physician as the mastermind. However, no one inside Haiti saw this doctor as anything but a useful idiot, intended to distract and hide the identity of the true perpetrators. He had no money of his own, no political support inside Haiti nor was there any realistic expectation he would be named president in the event of President Moise's departure or demise.

The F.B.I. and the Colombian National Police were brought in as consultants. As the investigation broadened, many prominent Haitian politicians and security people were interrogated and some even placed under arrest. At the same time, rival factions and families accused each other of being the masterminds behind the plot. The investigation was already faltering when another earthquake struck on August 14. The interim government proved impotent to respond and anarchy set in, with gangs in control of the streets, including the main road to the disaster area. Kidnapping surged once again. One month after the assassination, the investigation had stalled.

Chapter 42
Prelude to a Murder

To understand the Moise assassination, one needs to understand Haiti's recent political history. Involvement in Haitian affairs by the United States, both publicly and behind-the-scenes became quite entangled during the Duvalier dictatorship. The thinking in the State Department went something like this: With the Cold War raging, Cuba had gone Communist. Haiti was even more poor than Cuba. It was no time to entrust the reins of power to the whims of democracy. U.S. funds poured into Haiti – some to support Duvalier's instruments of power; the police, the army, and his private paramilitary, the TonTon Macoutes. Other dollars went to foreign aid programs, mostly "show and tell" housing projects for the displaced rural poor. The Duvaliers (Françoise, a.k.a. "Papa Doc" and his son Jean Claude, a.k.a. "Baby Doc") ruled Haiti from 1957 to 1988. After Baby Doc exiled himself to the south of France (with a sizable fortune), there was an international outcry for free and fair elections. In 1990, Jean Bertrand Aristide, a former priest and advocate for Haiti's poor, won the only free and fair election in Haiti's history up to that point. After two hundred years, democracy might finally have a chance.

Being an advocate for the poor in Haiti is not for the faint of heart! He had survived four assassination attempts. He was exiled after a coup by the army in 1990, returned to Haiti, largely through the diplomatic efforts of Bill Clinton, and then sent into exile again in 2004, after a coup spearheaded by paramilitary "rebels." Supporters of President Aristide suspected that the C.I.A. was involved. The Preval presidency that succeeded Aristide initiated substantial programs for Haiti's poor in health and education, but progress was derailed by the earthquake of 2010. Aristide's political party, Lavalas, was banned from the next two elections. As a result, turnout was extremely low – only twenty percent of the electorate turned out for the 2015 presidential election. Of this fraction, Jovenel Moise received only thirty percent of the vote in the first round – enough to make it to the runoff, but hardly an endorsement of broad popular support. So much for democracy...

Moise lacked not only popular support but also support from the elite families that traditionally controlled Haitian politics, with one important exception – former resident Michel Martelly. Martelly's entry into Haitian politics was curious. Prior to his election, his only claim to fame was as a crossdressing singer with the state name of Sweet Micky. In a runoff election, however, he had several factors in his favor – he was light-skinned, and his father was from a prominent family (he managed a gas company). His musical career made him quite popular with the sons and daughters of the elite. He also appeared to have the backing of former President Clinton, who headed the Interim Commission. Although he claimed solidarity with the poor, he ran on an anti-Aristide platform, promoting businesses and attempting to establish the army, which Aristide had disbanded. Barred from serving two consecutive terms, he chose Moise as his successor, hoping he would be popular with the poor because he was dark-skinned and came from the north rather than Port au Prince, which all Haitians know is controlled by the elite.

Rival parties disputed Moise's election, delaying his inauguration. As a result, he claimed he was owed another year in power. Failure to conduct senatorial elections allowed him to rule by decree his last year in office. When President Martelly's support faded and stories emerged that perhaps President Moise would investigate links between the Martelly Administration and drug cartels, rumors of assassination plots permeated the Presidential Palace.

Chapter 43
Follow the Money

I settled into my sofa, watching coverage of the Moise assassination on cable news. I had been retired now for eight years from the University of Miami Miller School of Medicine and had not been back to Haiti for the past two years, as a travel ban by the university prohibited my students from going there. Nevertheless, I couldn't quite escape my fascination with this story. Watching the news, it was difficult not to be bemused by the stumbling of the media – the "red herring" Haitian-American doctor with delusions of grandeur, the setup of the Colombian mercenaries, the curious absence of presidential security and the impotence of Haitian authorities to identify a mastermind, suggested an elaborate Babushka Doll that shielded the identity of those that plotted and executed the act.

For all the years that I worked in Haiti, I advised my students that to be successful as a healthcare provider in Haiti, it was not enough to just know medicine. If you wanted to help the people there, you had to know everything about them; their language, culture, economy, and particularly in the case of Haiti, their politics. That dictum was being put to the test by the Moise assassination.

"Why," I asked myself, "would someone devise such an elaborate plot to kill the president of the poorest nation in the hemisphere?" The obvious answers were money and its companion, power. What, then, were the coveted sources of this president's money and power? As I had come to learn during my time in Haiti, some were the more traditional, almost institutionalized parts of the Haitian political *modus operandi* – for example, bribes and kickbacks. In any autocratic state, if you want power and influence, you must pay for it. Without checks on the executive power, payments to the executive for power and influence were to be expected. That money, however, would flow to whoever held high office. What placed a target on President Moise's back were recent developments unique to Haiti, involving large amounts of new dollars. In no particular order, these included:

The Venezuelan gas subsidy. The Haitian economy is very dependent upon gasoline, more specifically, diesel. Diesel fuels the *tap-taps* that flood the streets of the capital, carrying workers to their jobs, women to their markets, and children to their schools. Buses transport people to and from the major cities. Large camions ply the highways and back roads, carrying people and produce to market and home again.

Hugo Chávez, in a show of solidarity with Haiti's poor, donated billions of dollars of diesel fuel to Haiti each year, under his Petrocaribe Program. For several years, this donation actually had its desired effect, bringing down inflation and lowering the cost of living of Haiti's poor. However, after Chávez died in 2013, direct fuel donations stopped, and the subsidy was changed to a cash equivalent. The distribution of this cash was controlled by the president and his ministers. Much of the political unrest that plagued Haiti just before the assassination was related to concerns among advocates for the poor that these funds were being diverted into the pockets of the rich and powerful. In fact, one consortium of businesses, including a company owned and managed by the future president, was accused of embezzling 3.8 billion dollars in fuel subsidies!

Foreign aid. After the 2010 earthquake, over twenty billion dollars of aid was pledged to Haiti from international banks and not-for-profit organizations. A committee, the Interim Relief Committee was formed, chaired by former President Bill Clinton, to develop a strategic plan to rebuild Haiti and see that the funds were fairly distributed. The committee soon became mired in bureaucracy, however, and after two years, its mandate expired. In truth, only a fraction of the money pledged to Haiti ever was actually donated. Of those dollars, only a minuscule amount was spent on projects intended to help the people – most of these dollars went to contractors under no-bid contracts or to purchase marginal land for construction of resettlement villages. Without planning for jobs and schools, these villages soon became ghost towns. Nevertheless, the control of these dollars shifted from the committee back to the president and his cabinet. However, because senatorial elections were delayed, no cabinet served during the last two years of President Moise's tenure in office.

Drugs. When the AIDS epidemic drove the final nail in the coffin of heroin as the street drug of choice in the 1980s, cocaine stepped forward to fill the void. Cocaine salt had been sniffed as a designer drug for some time, but in the 1980s – better living through chemistry – it was discovered that heating cocaine with water and bicarbonate of soda yielded a free base – a lipid soluble form that could be smoked, avoiding the problem of dirty needles. The fact that it was a lipid increased its absorption through the lipid-lined lungs and across the blood-brain barrier. "Crack" as it was called, therefore produced an intense but short-lived "high" and an all-consuming addiction. Plus, it was cheap – literally, money that grew on trees! A nickel bag of crack cost $5 on the streets of Miami – the same price for the basic services of a street prostitute, allowing cocaine use to soar among the poor, the homeless, sex workers, and their clients.

Colombia was the principal source of cocaine and Haiti proved to be a convenient way station for cocaine trafficking. Its airport has direct flights to Miami, New York, and Chicago. It also had plenty of poor people willing to act as "mules," swallowing cocaine-laden condoms to escape detection at customs. In addition, it had a long, unpatrolled coastline, providing speed boats with an alternative source of entry. There was also a steady traffic of cargo ships between Port-au-Prince and Miami, nominally transporting used bikes, clothing, and other items for the informal sector of Haiti's economy, but with ample storage in their holds and bilges for large quantities of cocaine. Finally, Haiti had the corruption and near-anarchy that allowed the cocaine cartels to operate with impunity.

The Cali Cartel surfaced openly in Haiti after the general's coup and continued to operate even after President Aristide was restored to power. I remember well the enclave of Colombian mansions behind a gated community on a knoll overlooking the road that connected Petionville with the airport. Everyone in Haiti and Little Haiti knew that Haiti had become a nexus for drug traffic, but the government under President Martelly and the National Police looked the other way. At one point, the Chief of Security under President Moise was a convicted drug trafficker! Drug money was also suspected to have permeated the Moise government. It was even the subject of a D.E.A. probe. Recently, supporters of President Moise claimed he was planning to crack down on drug cartels and the politicians who were working with them. The individuals involved in drug trafficking were reportedly the names on the list taken by the hit squad when they ransacked the president's estate. We have no way of knowing whether this rumor is true, whether it was concocted to rehabilitate the slain president's reputation or whether it was drafted to extort money from those on the list. No one knows for sure how much money was flowing from the cartels, but as anarchy descended upon Haiti, the time seemed right for Moise's rivals to claim their share of the pie.

Chapter 44
Ockham's Razor

According to stories posted on the Internet, mostly from Colombian and Dominican sources, it appears that one or two of the Colombians did confess to the assassination, although they claimed to be acting under direction of a Haitian Security official. The other Colombians claimed they were only there to serve a warrant that would allow for a new interim president. Evidently, the warrant is now in the hands of the investigators. The large amount of money the Colombians claim was discovered when they ransacked the president's home has not been found. Sufficient detail was provided in the confessions to lend them credence – a former Haitian Security Officer whose whereabouts is now unknown, ordered only one or two of the Colombians to open fire with a "take no prisoners" order – "Everyone in there, even the pets must die! There can be no witnesses!"

So, who killed Jovenel Moise? It's easier to say who did not. It was not simply a grudge killing. There were too many players involved and too much advance planning. Nor was it akin to the assassination of Julius Caesar – a group of high-minded senators fearing the fall of the Republic. Were that the case, an arrest of the president with a warrant would have sufficed. Likewise, this was not like the killing of Caligula by the Praetorian Guard, eliminating a despot that had clearly gone mad. Once again, his arrest would have sufficed and there was no need to bring in the Colombians.

In fourteenth century, the philosopher, Sir William of Ockham, proposed a rule of logic. When more than one possible solution to a problem exists, choose the simplest. When all the evidence was weighed, it was impossible to avoid the conclusion that the simplest solution was that the murder was about drugs and drug money. I ran this theory by Haitian American associates familiar with the workings of Haitian politics. "Drugs, drugs, drugs!" they all replied. The fact that the hit squad was predominantly ex-Colombian military and knew of a large amount of money in the president's home clearly opened the outer shell of this Babushka Doll.

The next doll was more difficult to open. The assassination could simply have been a Mafia-style payback for an exorbitant (in the minds of the cartels) extortion. Alternatively, perhaps the Colombians and their financiers had heard of the large amount of cash in the president's home. In that case, the motive would have been robbery, pure and simple. That does not explain, however, the Haitian connection – the issuance of a warrant, the Haitian security official who was calling the shots, the promise of shelter in the presidential palace and protection by the new president. The Colombians were clearly the intermediate agents of Moise's murder but the masterminds appeared to be within the Haitian government.

Who was most likely to benefit from the president's death? First on the list would have to be the prime minister, Ariel Henry. According to Haitian law, he would assume the presidency until elections could be held, with all the power and access to money that being the president of Haiti entailed. Only he could guarantee the Colombians the presidential palace as a haven or control the Haitian police and security forces.

But that left one more Babushka Doll to open. There may have been others, rich and powerful, who helped set up the elaborate ruse of the Colombians, recruited and financed by American firms. Sitting on my couch, this was about as far as I could take it. However, based on my knowledge of how they worked on the Agnes kidnapping, I was sure the F.B.I. would soon expose the entire conspiracy. It was only a matter of time…

Chapter 45
Déjà Vu

In the days following the assassination, Haiti shifted from near anarchy to total anarchy. Here's what total anarchy looks like – gangs divided up neighborhoods of Port-au-Prince, setting up roadblocks and demanding money for safe passage. Gangs in Haiti first emerged during another time of anarchy, when paramilitary groups descended on the capital to oust President Aristide. Known as *chimeres*, after the multi-headed monster of mythology, some saw themselves as civilian defense squads, intent on resisting the overthrow of the President. Others were clearly opportunists, taking advantage of the chaos to raid, loot, kidnap, or otherwise seek revenge on the wealthy elite whom they blamed for the attempted and ultimately successful coup. Now, similarly, some gangs saw themselves as protectors of their neighborhoods, in a time when the police could not be trusted. Others, however, were clearly taking advantage of the vacuum of authority to make money, either by extortion, ransom, or drug smuggling.

The price of goods and gasoline soared, as did the number of kidnappings. For the month of September 2021 alone, more than six hundred kidnappings were reported. Large swaths of the capital had no food, electricity, or safe water. Some people languished, starving and sick, in their neighborhoods, hoping for some form of deliverance. Others tried to escape, either by land or by sea. Those who left by land hoped to make it to the cities up Rue Nationale to the north. In bus convoys, they risked the roadblocks and burning tire barricades at every small town along the way. Many were forced to abandon their buses, leaving them stranded far from their homes. Those who chose to leave by sea faced even greater peril – the number who drowned during the seven-hundred-mile journey to South Florida in makeshift sailboats will never be known. What is known, according to the United States Immigration and Naturalization Service, is that in the year 2022, eight thousand Haitians were captured at sea, in the Bahamas, and Cuba and sent back to Haiti. A year after the assassination, the sea route appears to be the preferred attempt to escape Haiti – in June 2022, a sailboat with about 150 Haitians went aground just south of Miami. Failing to make land, they will most likely be sent back to Haiti. A few days later, seventeen Haitians died when their boat capsized in the Bahamas. Now the arrival of overcrowded handmade sailboats packed with desperate Haitians on South Florida's beaches is a daily occurrence.

On August 14, five weeks after the assassination, Haiti's southern peninsula was struck by a 7.2 magnitude earthquake, followed shortly thereafter by tropical storm Grace. It was almost like Mother Nature had joined forces with the assassination conspirators. There were no major population centers involved, just small cities, towns, and villages spread out over hundred miles. The few functioning hospitals on the peninsula were overwhelmed. Over the next week, the death toll officially climbed to 2,200, but most organizations working in the quake zone estimated that the actual number of dead was probably ten times that. Over two hundred thousand people were without food, safe water, health care, or shelter.

Making matters worse, the gangs that blocked access to the main road into the southern peninsula, in a neighborhood called Martissant, forced the severely injured to be evacuated by helicopter or by boat, to hospitals as far away as Mirebelais. International agencies had no confidence in the dysfunctional Haitian government and Haitians, tainted by the experiences of the 2010 earthquake, had no confidence in the international agencies. Cholera and other waterborne illnesses were soon surging in the earthquake zone.

The investigation into President Moise's assassination has been suspended. Few expect it will ever resume. In fact, a year after the assassination, the murder has faded from the country's collective memory. No mastermind has been identified, interrogated, or jailed. The prime minister was called to be interviewed by the prosecutors but declined the invitation. They in turn, after calling for his arrest, have either resigned or have been terminated. Disappointingly, the F.B.I. has been silent on the subject.

Over and above the political and social upheaval caused by the assassination, Haiti is now undergoing a moral upheaval. The old folks still struggle to cling to their belief that all this – the assassination, the quake, gangs, kidnappings, and cholera – must be God's will. Somehow, in ways we cannot now see, good will come from it all. The next generations, however, at least in the capital, are losing their faith and losing their hope. And as the wise words of the old folks in Kreyol go, "*Lespwa fe viv, lespwa fe mouri!*" Hope makes us live! Hope unfulfilled, however, makes us die!

Chapter 46
A Bridge Too Far

Sunday, September 19 2021

For Martine, sitting on the banks of the Rio Grande was strangely reminiscent of Haiti in happier times – people bathing and washing their clothes in the river, while children frolicked in the shallow waters, seemingly carefree. Everywhere, there were throngs of people speaking Kreyol, exchanging news, laughing, and sharing plans on where they would go after they cleared Customs into the United States. She hoped the rumors she had heard were true – that the latest earthquake in Haiti would move the United States Government to grant Haitians abroad something called *TPS.* Cousins who happened to be in Miami after the last quake had been granted TPS – officially, Temporary Protected Status – and would take her in if only she could get across the border.

Martine was sixteen when the 2010 earthquake struck. Her life was spared because she was outside learning dance steps from her girlfriends while all the buildings around her collapsed. However, she lost her parents that evening and perhaps two brothers, who were never found. She spent two years in a tent city, sharing her tent with other orphaned girls. When told she would be relocated to a resettlement village at the base of Mont Kabrit, a barren, desolate place in the desert to the north of the city, she decided it was time to leave Haiti.

She got a job cleaning crew quarters on a freighter bound for Caracas. From there, she caught a bus to Brazil, finding work as a maid in a beach resort northeast of Rio De Janeiro.

She liked Brazil at first – the life of the people there seemed a lot like the life of the people in Haiti. However, when the COVID pandemic crushed the tourist economy, she was let go. A group of fellow Haitian expatriates decided to band together and take buses to the US / Mexican border. Under the Trump Administration, she knew that the chances that she would get into the United States were small. She spent a year in a makeshift camp close to the border until rumors spread through the camp that, as a result of another earthquake, TPS for Haitians might be reinstated. To be ready, just in case a miracle happened, she joined thousands of other Haitian expatriates at the Rio Grande near the border town of Del Rio, Texas.

After Mass that Sunday, Martine took her small sack with a few clothes and a small box that contained her savings and headed for the Del Rio bridge. She bought a couple of bottles of water and a few *empanadas* from a roadside vendor, then took off her sandals and walked across the shallow water flowing over a dam under the bridge. She could then honestly say she had made it to the United States, even if it were only on a grassy embankment whose perimeter was heavily guarded by the Border Patrol.

She sat down on a towel she had taken with her from the hotel in Brazil. There was an excited buzz amongst the crowd on both sides of the river, that something was about to happen. President Trump had totally shut down the border, not only for undocumented migrants looking for work but also for children and families seeking asylum. The new administration had already changed policy concerning children and tried to deal with asylum-seekers from Central America by shipping them to empty military bases, allowing them to stay there while their claims were being processed. Martine made a rosary (or was it Erzili's veve?) out of the small pebbles on the river's edge and whispered the required sequence of prayers over and over, hoping the Virgin was listening.

The talk among the expatriates centered on what would make the best asylum claim. Clearly, neither displacement by the last earthquake, loss of home or family, nor sheer misery would qualify – economic or social claims would be rejected. The consensus was that the best hope for a successful claim came with some threat of bodily harm, either by the police or by the gangs that controlled the streets in the poorest neighborhoods. There was more than a little truth in this claim, particularly for young women. Martine had witnessed it herself during nights in the tent cities when police, nominally there to protect them, cajoled, harassed, and threatened women to submit to their desires.

What Martine did not know was that Haitians were always treated differently when it came to immigration. Whether it was their Blackness or the fear that these desperately poor would unleash a crime wave on our cities, the rules were different for Haitians. Be it the internment in the 1980s of the boat people, for decades without a hearing, in the Krome Avenue Detention Center, west of Miami, the "wet foot / dry foot" policy that favored Cuban refugees over Haitians, the interdiction and return of Haitian boats by the coast guard patrolling just off the Haitian coast, the refusal by the State Department to allow Haitians, even those severely injured, to come to this country after the 2010 earthquake or the Obama policy of deporting "criminals" whose only offense might be a traffic ticket. It was clear, as a matter of policy, that "give me your tired, your poor, your huddled masses yearning to be free" did not apply to Haitians!

On the day that Martine was saying her rosary, the Department of Homeland Security declared that they were instituting a policy of massive air deportation back to Haiti. The rights of asylum-seekers were suspended under something called Title 42, the COVID exemption. No matter that there was no real functioning Haitian government to negotiate the return of these expatriates and no plan to treat them humanely when they returned to Haiti. Nor did it matter that the latest earthquake created thousands more homeless and injured who needed help and hoped they might also apply for TPS. What did matter was that the border optics needed to be sanitized.

A Border Patrol officer on horseback ordered Martine in Spanish to gather her things and follow him, so that she could begin the process of applying for asylum. She was taken to a bus and transported to an airfield about fifty miles away. The following morning, she was loaded onto a plane and flown to Port-au-Prince. Upon arrival, she was welcomed by the prime minister (the same Prime Minister suspected of being involved in the assassination) in a pre-recorded speech, given a plate of rice, beans, and chicken, as well as cash (reports range from $25 to $100). She was also given a "hygiene kit" containing toilet paper, a toothbrush, and soap. The kit was emblazoned with the USAID logo and labeled "a gift from the American people." She was then released to the streets. Over the next week, thousands of Haitian expatriates met the same fate (estimates range from two thousand to seven thousand deportees). The special ambassador to Haiti resigned over the treatment of Haitian refugees and four United Nations agencies condemned the deportation policy. In spite of these protests, the flights kept on coming.

The acrid smoke of burning rubber burned her eyes as she left the airport terminal. She clutched her hygiene kit and small sack of belongings close to her chest as she tried to find a path out to the road into the city – not that she knew what she would do there, but where else was she to go? Then out of the crowd, a young man approached her. Dressed in pressed jeans, a vest, and a gold chain around his neck, he hardly appeared to be Haitian. He spoke Kreyol, however, as he pulled Martine aside.

"Cheri, I know a gentleman who needs a housekeeper. Are you interested…?"

Chapter 47
L'enfer

The twelve staff workers (eleven Americans and one Canadian) of the Christian Aid Ministries boarded their bus at their headquarters in Tintayen the morning of October 16 2021, for what they thought would be a routine visit to the Providence de Dieu orphanage in the Ganthier District, about fifteen miles away. Never mind the reports of kidnappings erupting all around Port-au-Prince, this delivery of bedclothes and Bibles seemed so routine that the group brought five of their children with them, including an eight-month-old! Prior to the 2010 earthquake, Tintayen was a desolate, barren, uninhabited place. It became infamous in the minds of Haitians after the earthquake as the site of mass graves of earthquake victims and a large resettlement camp for families displaced by the earthquake. Land, always a precious commodity in Haiti, was available there, although at the time it was devoid of infrastructure. Christian Aid Ministries purchased property there as the headquarters for their expanded presence in Haiti after the quake.

The bus headed across a desert-like landscape to join National Road 3 near the base of Morn Kabrit, then headed south to a small stretch of the road where the edge of the desert blends with the suburban outskirts of Croix des Bouquets. There is a row of orphanages there, including La Maison du

Providence de Dieu. It took little time to distribute the bed clothes. Most of the day was spent giving each orphan a Bible, in French, and reading passages with the children together. It was a morale-booster for the Christian Aid Ministries team who had only recently returned to Haiti after being recalled home to Ohio for safety concerns.

The group sang hymns with the children before climbing back on their bus for the trip back to headquarters. To everyone's shock, however, when the gates of the orphanage opened, they were surrounded by a large group of youths carrying semi-automatic weapons. In a matter of minutes, the bus was commandeered, and the missionaries whisked away to a network of safe houses. The price demanded for their release? $17 million.

The practice of kidnapping has now come full circle since the abduction of Agnes in 2005. That kidnapping was one of many small-scale crimes that arose with the impotence of the National Police following the removal of President Aristide. Kidnapping is now on a grander scale and much more organized. Nevertheless, there are lessons to be learned from the story of Agnes's ordeal. First, there had to be an insider in the Christian Aid Mission kidnappings – someone who could tip off the gangs as to the exact itinerary and plans of the group on October 16. Second, the event was clearly carefully planned, with the targets identified, sufficient weaponized force mustered, and safe houses identified, where the missionaries could be hidden.

Less well-appreciated, both then and now, was the role that the U.S. State Department played in creating the anarchy required for kidnapping to flourish in Haiti in the first place. Policies that supported right-wing autocrats that lacked broad popular support began first with the Duvaliers and continued under Presidents G.W. Bush and Trump. In 2004, elements of the army that President Aristide had disbanded infiltrated across the Dominican border, terrorized the countryside, and descended upon the capital. While the role the C.I.A. played in this "rebellion" has never been clarified, we do know that when the United States Ambassador told President Aristide that the United States could not guarantee his safety, he chose to leave the country. At least, however, at that time, there was a functioning U.S. Embassy and an F.B.I. presence to protect U.S. citizens. Indeed, the proscription against kidnapping foreigners that took root in the wake of Agnes' rescue held until just recently.

The Trump administration's policy towards Haiti was essentially to let it rot. At the time of the assassination of president Moise, there was no U.S. ambassador or F.B.I. presence in the country. A request to the Biden Administration to send U.S. troops to establish order was declined, setting the stage for complete anarchy and the rise of gangs as pseudo-governance. As a result, kidnappings have expanded to include not only individuals but groups representing entities that might provide extraordinary ransoms.

After the assassination, gangs first surfaced at critical intersections in the Martisant neighborhood of Carrefour, setting up barricades and demanding payment for safe passage from all who tried to travel to or from the Southern Peninsula. Since then, as gas prices rose, food and water became scarce and police protection evaporated, gangs metastasized throughout the city and its environs. At this writing, eighty percent of greater Port au Prince is controlled by gangs. With no solution to the security crisis in sight, the influence of gangs will surely extend out of the capital and into the countryside.

Gang leaders frequently held prior positions with the police or were openly tied to the drug trade. Some have political ambitions, while others appear opaquely tied to political parties and the political elite, who depended on gangs to protect their assets. Their power is based on the clandestine purchase of extraordinary amounts of firearms. They operate as warlords or neighborhood Mafia bosses, demanding tribute from all in exchange for "protection." In the district of Ganthier, where the goatherd Michel hailed from and where the Christian Aid Ministries abduction unfolded, even the goatherds are now being taxed, paying so much per head for the number of goats they herd!

Women are particularly vulnerable in these troubled times. There is nothing to stop a gang member armed with a weapon from coercing young women and girls into sexual servitude. This servitude may range from forced cohabitation to an outright rape at the whim of a gang member. Parents and loved ones are powerless to stop this abuse. To make matters worse, the women who are victims of these rapes are frequently stigmatized, ostracized, and dragged against their will into long-term sexual exploitation.

The political vacuum that led to the rise of gangs also expanded the role of non-governmental organizations in providing social services. Some commentators have even called the present situation in Haiti the "NGO state." These organizations vary widely in size, funding, and mission, ranging from large international entities like the Red Cross and UNICEF, to small missions organized by individual churches (overwhelmingly evangelical Protestant) with home bases in the United States. Funding for missionary activities traditionally came from individual donations. During the G. W. Bush Administration, however, faith-based organizations received a considerable portion of U.S. foreign aid to Haiti.

There are so many faith-based groups working in Haiti that it is difficult to generalize about their missions. Many, if not most, simply want to follow the teachings of their faith to feed the hungry, clothe the naked, and give shelter to the less fortunate. Caring for orphans is frequently included in these missions. Orphans are a growth industry in Haiti. They are found throughout the country, although in the countryside most orphans have simply been taken in by extended family. The phenomenon of institutional orphans, however, is unique to Haiti's cities and has been exacerbated by the forces that promote internal migration away from the countryside and into cities that have no social safety net.

Orphans tug at the heartstrings of people of goodwill and prove lucrative from the fundraising perspective. When large orphanages are home to hundreds of children, it becomes relatively easy to generate the kind of numbers necessary to satisfy funding agencies on a large scale. There is a dark side to orphan care, however. Orphans are easily exploitable children, particularly if there is no government agency overseeing the orphanages and the missions running them. Even if one ignores the most egregious cases, such as the missionaries from Idaho who, after the 2010 earthquake, bought children from desperate parents and attempted to sex-traffic them through the Dominican Republic, the opportunities for secret, subtle exploitation of children exist in the very nature of institutionalized orphanages and their administration. This is particularly true when they are administered by foreigners who may or may not have the orphans' best interests at heart. In fact, in 2019, a worker at the Christian Aid Ministries headquarters in Haiti voluntarily confessed and sought forgiveness for sexually abusing young boys. Most Americans are blind to these cases of abuse. They are, however, common knowledge, spread by word of mouth among Haitians, eroding the moral high ground of the missions and providing an excuse for gangs to justify kidnappings.

While the kidnapping of Americans grabbed the international media's attention, crimes against Haitians never rose to the international public's consciousness. These crimes, including rape, along with the shortage of food, water, and gasoline did far more to create a milieu of hopelessness and life a living hell among the people than did the missionary kidnappings.

Epilogue

As 2021 ends, Michel is now thirty-four years old. He still works as a custodian in the Miami-Dade County schools – his life changed forever, not in a way he could have foreseen, by a few minutes of furtive conversation with Agnes. His two sons attend public school in Miami; the oldest will soon graduate! Frustrated with life in Miami, Cheri returned to Lamardelle to be close to her mother. Michel sends them remittances every month. He regrets that they are no longer together but accepts their separation as a price he must pay for doing the right thing. Omart is retired from the F.B.I. but still visits his friend, Michel, regularly and takes him to sporting events. Being Haitian, Michel prefers *futbol* (soccer) over football, baseball, and basketball.

Dr. Andre Vulcain took early retirement from Miami's Department of Family Medicine in 2015. He managed to scrape together some donations from Haitian-American colleagues and, along with his own contributions, continued traveling to Cap Haitian on a regular basis for the next six years. His beloved training program there now is being forced to shut down due to lack of funds. However, he is working with Partners in Health to expand family medicine training to other hospitals throughout the country.

After more than two months of captivity, the kidnapped missionaries have either been released or escaped. Their identity and the circumstances of their release were originally tightly guarded secrets. Three days later, however, they posed for photographs for the international media. They told an incredible tale of escape in the middle of the night, after a sign, they claim, from God, and a ten-hour trek through brambles and thistles, in which they navigated, using stars as their guides, to a mountain (from the photographs released, clearly the infamous Morn Kabrit). There, they borrowed the cell phone of a passer-by to call the authorities, who secured them and quickly repatriated them to the United States. The media accepted this story unquestioningly, and who can blame them? We all love happy endings and the successful escape of the missionaries brought closure to the kidnapping issue for most here in the U.S. However, this story warrants a microscope of skepticism. It strains credulity that the guards would neither hear their opening of a supposedly barricaded gate nor pursue them during the ten-hour time they claim it took to walk to their rescue. The moon was waxing, making all but the brightest stars and planets invisible and the North Star – the only fixed object in the nighttime sky – is a third-order magnitude star that is difficult to see for the untrained eye in even the clearest and darkest of nights. There is nothing at Morn Kabrit but a highway, most likely patrolled by gangs. These incongruities force the critical observer to consider an alternative explanation – that the story was concocted or the escape staged to hide the fact that ransom was paid.

Meanwhile, kidnappings and extortion of Haitians continue at an astounding rate (approaching eight hundred between September and December 2021) and there is no end in sight for more kidnappings and shortages of food, water, and gas. Drugs and drug money flush through the capital like water down a toilet – the difference now being that the pay-offs are going to gang leaders as well as politicians. Murders, either of opposing gang members or innocent bystanders, have surged. Over eight hundred victims were killed in Cite Soleil during one week in July 2022.

The American policy of forced repatriation continues. As a result, more desperate Haitians are taking to the sea, hoping to make it to South Florida. Calls for the prime minister to resign have been ignored and elections have been indefinitely postponed. The investigation into the murder of President Moise is suspended.

Unfortunately, the recent graduates of the Haitian medical school assigned to the community health program to fulfil their social service obligation were not deployed by the Ministry of Health, so Medishare's Maternity Centers currently lack physician coverage. The social service program will hopefully resume in January. The trauma hospital in Port au Prince that my colleague, Dr. Barth Green, worked so hard to establish is now closed for security reasons.

This continuing cascade of misfortune brings us back to the question of whether there is meaning to be found in any of this. Hopefully, the vignettes presented here will inform reflections on this issue. For Haitians, the Kreyol answer to the question of finding meaning in catastrophe is simply that it is God's will and somehow good will come, eventually, from every misfortune. There is a corollary, however, to this world view that is less well appreciated; if good is to come from misfortune, we must create that good, no matter how improbable the odds that we will succeed. As the Kreyol proverb succinctly captures – on the other side of the mountain there are always more mountains to climb! Unfortunately, if we look at the heroes and villains at work in Haiti now, determining its fate, the villains have the upper hand!

That said, good is coming from some of this, at least when it comes to health – the only issue on which I can write with some authority. The response by the University of Miami Miller School of Medicine to the 2010 earthquake was arguably its finest hour; over six thousand operations were performed in the field hospital set up under the tents set up by Marie, including two thousand amputations!

After the 2010 earthquake, Haiti's medical school and teaching hospital were moved out of the capital and into the countryside to the small provincial city of Mirebalais – the pragmatic argument that it made no sense to rebuild near a fault line was coupled with the philosophic apology that medical training in Haiti ought to occur not in the city, but out in the countryside, where ninety percent of the people live. When gangs blocked access to the southern peninsula after the earthquake of 2021, trauma victims were airlifted to the new hospital; the only accessible hospital with the capacity to deal with this catastrophe.

Medishare's mobile clinics, home visits, bleach distribution, and vaccination programs in the Central Plateau continue, with the Haitian staff trained and inspired by Marie. Marie, before she died, also initiated an "orphans and vulnerable children's program," which, as opposed to institutionalizing orphans in orphanages run by foreigners, pays family members who take in orphans and children of parents dying of AIDS a monthly food allowance and the cost of sending that child to school. Over a hundred children are currently enrolled. However, the costs of all these operations have recently increased dramatically, because of the increase in the cost of fuel, coupled with deflation of the Haitian currency. As a result, these programs are at risk of being curtailed.

These small victories are occurring throughout Haiti, without fanfare, wherever Haitians are trained and empowered to take healthcare into their own hands. Although not alone in this approach, Partners in Health deserves credit for taking it to a national scale. Whether, in the cosmic calculus, these victories justify the disasters which spawned them, I leave to all of us to ponder…